F
Denholtz

W9-CLD-756

Denholtz, Roni
  Marquis in a minute

HESSTON PUBLIC LIBRARY
T 55035
WITHDRAWN

5/14/07   **DATE DUE**

AUG 1 3 2007			
SEP 0 5 '07			
3-12-08 WC			
5-1-08 HH			
7-1-08 SV			
	WITHDRAWN		

F
Denholtz

MARQUIS IN
A MINUTE

Other books by Roni Denholtz:

Negotiating Love
Lights of Love
Somebody to Love

F
Denholtz
T 55035

MARQUIS IN A MINUTE

•

Roni Denholtz

Hesston Public Library
P.O. Box 640
110 East Smith
Hesston, KS 67062

AVALON BOOKS
NEW YORK

© Copyright 2007 by Roni Paitchel Denholtz
All rights reserved.
All the characters in this book are fictitious,
and any resemblance to actual persons,
living or dead, is purely coincidental.
Published by Thomas Bouregy & Co., Inc.
160 Madison Avenue, New York, NY 10016

Library of Congress Cataloging-in-Publication Data

Denholtz, Roni S.
   Marquis in a minute / Roni Denholtz.
      p. cm.
   ISBN 978-0-8034-9837-2 (acid-free paper)
   I. Title.

PS3554.E5314M37 2007
813'.54—dc22

                                        2007004989

PRINTED IN THE UNITED STATES OF AMERICA
ON ACID-FREE PAPER
BY HADDON CRAFTSMEN, BLOOMSBURG, PENNSYLVANIA

For Christina Lynn Whited and Karen Bryan:
Not only great critique partners but
wonderful friends as well!

Chapter One

In what seemed like a minute, Andrew Pennington became the third man to hold the Marquis of Whitbury title that day.

He had rarely considered the possibility that this could happen and had always deemed it highly unlikely.

The night his life changed so abruptly, he was sitting at Green's Gentleman's Club with two friends, a glass of brandy in his hand. It was a rainy evening in April. Having just come in from the chilly, wet and dismal weather, Andrew was glad enough to sit down with his closest friend Edward, and Henry, another acquaintance.

Now Edward raised his brandy snifter. "To the memory of your Uncle Elias," he said solemnly.

"To Elias." Andrew and Henry raised their glasses. The brandy slipped smoothly down Andrew's throat, and instantly warmed his stomach. He held the glass, swirling the dark ruby liquid.

"May he rest in peace," Andrew added. After a moment, he raised his eyes to his friends. "It's hard to believe the old man is gone."

"Yes, he has been around for all our lives," Edward said. "It seemed he would live forever."

"Does he have much family?" Henry asked. Henry, who had gone to Oxford with Andrew and Edward, had recently arrived from his family home in northern England and was not well acquainted with many of the aristocratic families in London. "Aside from his son Cyril, that is?"

"No. My father was his only—younger—brother," Andrew said, sighing. "When my father and mother died there was no one but Elias, cousin Cyril, my sisters and I." He said the words sadly, the familiar ache welling up inside of him. He still missed his father's jovial face and his mother's more serene countenance. It had been only three years since the carriage accident that took their lives.

"And Elias' wife died long ago," Edward added.

"No, there's not much family left—just my two elder sisters and I," reiterated Andrew, taking another sip of the warming drink. "And of course, Millicent and Elizabeth are both married now and have their own families to tend to. I sent off letters to them about Uncle Elias' demise this afternoon."

"There will be few to mourn him, I presume," Henry said.

"That's true." Andrew sighed. "Although perhaps you didn't know—coming from the north country—but most of society did know Uncle Elias. Not merely because he lived a long time—or because he was the

Marquis of Whitbury. It's a very old title, and the family's always been wealthy. No, he was known for the way he increased the family coffers. Partly from wise investments and partly because the old man was extraordinarily . . . well, everyone knew Uncle Elias was as tightfisted as they come."

"Now, Andrew," Edward said, with a small laugh, "we should not speak ill of the dead."

"Uncle Elias wouldn't think it ill of me to speak so," Andrew protested. "He was quite proud of his reputation. He used to say to my father and I, 'Look to me as an example of one who knows how to manage money!' My father, however, was more relaxed about money and knew how to spend wisely while still having funds to enjoy life." Andrew paused, stretching his legs closer to the glowing fire in the hearth. The heat penetrated his boots and clothes and was quite comforting. Outside, rain pelted the windows with a sharp report. He twirled the brandy glass once more.

"And when I would say to him, yes, uncle, your business acumen is unparalleled, he would laugh. He would say, in the proudest of voices, 'That's a certainty, boy!' It became somewhat of a joke, something we always said to each other." His voice dropped. "In fact, I said it for the last time to Uncle only this morning, when his doctor summoned me, fearing the end was near." It was comforting to think he had brought Uncle Elias a bit of amusement at the very end.

"It sounds as if he took great pride in being miserly," Henry stated, with a sip.

"Ah, yes," Andrew agreed. "And he got more tightfisted after Cyril, my cousin, came of age."

"Why is that?" Henry asked.

"Hmmph." This from Edward, with a grin. He swiftly drained his glass.

Laughter broke out down the hall. The nasty weather had driven many of the town's gentlemen inside this evening, and the club was more crowded than usual. The small room where Andrew sat with Edward and Henry was one of the few not full of gentlemen drinking, looking over the paper, or wagering on card games.

News of the old marquis' death had spread quickly this day. People were amazed, since Elias had hung on so long despite failing health these past ten years. Andrew knew for a fact that some of the ton were already laying wagers on how long it would be before cousin Cyril went through the family fortune Elias had amassed.

Henry was looking at Andrew with raised eyebrows.

"As for cousin Cyril . . ." Andrew shrugged. He had never cared for his self-centered older cousin, the only child of the marquis and the marquis' late wife. "Uncle Elias kept a tight rein on the family coffers, especially when he realized Cyril had a penchant for gambling."

"I have heard he enjoys wagering," Henry said, nodding.

"He went on a tour of the continent several years ago and went through the money Uncle Elias gave him with great speed," Andrew said. "After that, Elias ordered him back to England and kept a close watch on what he spent, only doling out the bare minimum to Cyril."

"Of which he gambled most of that away," Edward said with disgust. "And he has a fondness for drink as well. It has always amazed me that he managed to get himself engaged to Isobel Newmont—one of the most beautiful young women to grace a ballroom in recent years."

"No surprise really," Andrew said. As he placed his glass on a side table, it clinked against the polished wood. "Cyril was the heir to the marquisdom. And now he is the marquis."

"Hmm, yes," Edward said, "still—"

Sudden noise from down the hall interrupted his words. As Andrew listened, he recognized his cousin Cyril's voice, pitched unnaturally loud, above the others.

"Yes, I *am* the marquis! At last!" More noise, and then, "A toast to meself—the new Marquis of Whit–bureee!"

Andrew pictured his cousin raising his glass and downing it in one gulp. It sounded as if it wasn't his first drink of the night. No surprise there, either.

He glanced at Edward, grimacing. "So much for keeping the good name of Whitbury nice and clean," he said, disgust edging his voice. "That was another priority of my uncle's. I suppose now we will hear stories daily of Cyril's wines and wagers."

Both his friends laughed.

"Farewell, friends . . . I must see to more funeral arrangements!" Cyril was fairly shouting now.

Andrew shuddered. Cyril didn't have to sound so gay about it. Cyril might have resented the old man's tightfisted ways, but Elias was his father, and due a certain amount of respect upon his death. Andrew knew Elias had been a man of his word and though tightfisted, he had taken excellent care of his lands and his tenants. He never spent an unnecessary shilling; but if a repair was needed, he saw to it swiftly.

Andrew could only imagine what would happen now that Cyril was taking charge.

"I do hope my cousin cares for the estates properly," he said, his voice taking on a note of worry. "I would hate to see him neglect the tenants and land so that he could place a wager—"

The voices from the hall grew closer.

"My cousin? . . . Yes . . . I will see him before I leave." Cyril's voice was definitely slurred. "Andrew . . ."

Cyril appeared in the doorway to the room where Andrew lounged with his friends. His body rocked back and forth, and he put out a hand to brace himself. "Cousin . . . Andrew," he said, somewhat pompously, his words slurred.

Andrew had seen his cousin only hours before at Whitbury House here in London, where both had been summoned to Elias' bedside. When Elias passed on, Cyril had seemed more gleeful than sorrowful, and it appeared he was celebrating the old man's demise.

"Yes?" Andrew responded to his cousin's words, striving to keep his face neutral and not disgusted.

There was a crackling noise from the fireplace as a piece of wood broke off, and Andrew smelled the charred wood.

Cyril hesitated, a foggy look overtaking his round face. His cheeks were quite red, and his eyes appeared dulled. "Can't remember what the devil—ah, yes, that's it." He rubbed his hands together. "The old man . . . my father—" He hiccupped. Andrew thought he heard a snort from Edward or Henry.

"Yes?" Andrew asked, his voice colder. Cyril was quite obviously foxed.

"The old man kicked the bucket, did ya know that?" Cyril was positively beaming.

"Yes, I did." Andrew stood up and approached Cyril. "The doctor summoned me this morning, remember? I was in the house with you when he passed on." A puff of smoke wafted towards them from the fireplace.

"Passed on. Yes. That's a . . . nice way of puttin' it," Cyril said. "Cousin Andrew, I believe the . . . old man wished for you to have his pocket watch as a . . . token"—Cyril hiccupped again—"He knew you . . . like to carry them. I wilsh . . . will remember to give it to you. Have to get on home, complete some more arrangements before the night is done."

"I will be honored to take the watch," Andrew replied solemnly. He studied Cyril, who continued to sway in the doorway. "I say, cousin, you appear to be rather foxed tonight." That was an understatement. Again, there was a snort behind him. "Do you want me to accompany you home?" Andrew certainly had no wish to do so; but he could not imagine how Cyril, who liked to drive his own curricle at a fast clip, would get home safely in this rain.

"No, no, I plan to stop at . . ." He looked confused once more. "I say, I believe I was . . . yes, I was planning to stop at Isobel's home. Have not . . . seen her . . . yet today. I shall walk. I ordered my personal carriage to be . . . to be . . . painted with the family crest." Again he beamed.

"So soon?" Andrew blurted out. Uncle Elias wasn't even in his grave and Cyril was making changes.

Cyril's ruddy cheeks grew redder. "Yes," he said, his voice becoming haughty. "I am the marquis now—it is my right."

"Well, perhaps I should go along with you." Studying his cousin, Andrew decided he had never seen Cyril so deep in his cups. "You are foxed, cousin Cyril; it may be dangerous for you to be walking about." In his confused state Cyril might not go to the correct house.

"I am a marquis; I can do as I please," Cyril snapped. "You, cousin Andrew . . . are nothing but the son of a second son of a marquis. A gentleman, no more." His face took on a sneer. "Watch yourself, cousin, if you want to be included in my celebrations after the . . . after the funeral."

Andrew had no desire to be included in any celebrations of Cyril's ever. "As you wish," he told his cousin coldly.

"Cyril, you really should listen to Andrew," Edward interrupted. "The weather tonight is beastly; one of us can bring you home. My home is only a few houses away from yours." Wind whistled, rattling the window as Edward spoke, as if for emphasis. "In the morning you will have slept it off, then you can go to visit your intended."

"She will probably not appreciate seeing you thus," Henry pointed out.

Cyril made a motion with his hand as if to strike them all down. "Enough! I am done listening to you. You all sound like a group of old women." He straightened, slowly, and Andrew observed he still wavered. "I am a marquis," he repeated in his most haughty voice. "I will do what I please."

His speech ended with another hiccup, which measurably detracted from any dramatic effect.

"I will see you on the morrow, then, cousin," Andrew said, and returned to his seat.

"Yes." Cyril turned and, unsteadily, left the doorway. As he walked down the hall, Andrew heard him mutter, "I am the marquis . . . the old man is gone!" followed by a gleeful chuckle.

Andrew cast a glance at Edward, then Henry. The two were sitting up in their chairs, sardonic looks on their faces.

"Well, he is wasting no time in taking over his duties," Edward said sarcastically.

"I did not expect him to celebrate so blatantly," Andrew said, sighing. "It does seem disrespectful of Uncle Elias." He stood up again and went to stand closer to the fireplace.

"Yes, well, apparently he has no concern for the mourning conventions," Henry said. "It is a shame to see the title pass into the hands of someone with so little . . . so little—"

"Maturity?" asked Andrew.

"Precisely."

They were silent for a moment. Then Andrew added, "He has had far too much to drink. I hope he gets to his fiancée's house in one piece. *If* he reaches the correct house."

"In his state, I would not be surprised if her family threw him out on his ear," Edward said. He stood up and went to stand by Andrew, leaning against the fireplace mantle.

"She has a brother who is not much better," Andrew pointed out.

"Ah, then perhaps he will look after him," Henry said.

Andrew shrugged. "Well, we offered to help."

"Now," Edward said, looking about for a pack of cards, "are you still interested in a game of chance?"

Andrew suspected his friend was trying to lighten the atmosphere. His own taste ran to card games wherein he and his friends wagered lightly; a bottle of wine, perhaps, or a luncheon. He had never participated in the heavy gambling his cousin enjoyed. The sort of expensive wagers for money or family heirlooms that Uncle Elias had halted when he learned of them. The kind of thing that, he supposed, Cyril was now going to indulge in with frequency.

Andrew and his friends were joined by Edward's younger brother Lawrence, and spent a pleasant hour playing cards and discussing politics.

When they finished they sat and relaxed. Andrew took out his pocket watch to check the time. It was a quarter hour past ten o'clock.

As he pocketed the watch, he heard a sudden commotion. A servant went rushing down the hall; then another.

"I will see what is happening," Lawrence volunteered. He leaped up and hurried down the hall.

Weariness had set in. Andrew got up, and stretched. "It has been a long day, my friends. I believe I will return home."

"A good idea," Edward said. "You have been occupied all day with your uncle, and his arrangements."

They could hear raised voices, and more footsteps in the hall. Exclamations ensued. "Gad!" someone cried out. And another, "We warned him!"

An uneasy sensation clutched at Andrew in the vicinity of his stomach. He tried to shake it off.

"I will see you day after tomorrow?" he said to Edward and Henry.

Lawrence burst into the room.

"Andrew!"

"Yes?" Seeing the young man's look of shock, Andrew's pulse quickened.

"Cyril is dead!" Lawrence cried.

As Lawrence said the words, two older men followed him into the room.

"Dead?" Andrew stared at Lawrence, then the other men, his entire body growing cold.

Lawrence indicated the two men. They wore overcoats splattered with water, and their fine boots were covered in mud. "Lord Fornay and Sir Chanders found him in the pond not a hundred yards from here!"

The gentlemen had removed their hats. "I am sorry," Lord Fornay said with dignity. "We left the club minutes ago; when we were passing the pond the horses acted skittish, and we observed something floating. We stopped the carriage and fished out your cousin."

Their wet clothes gave evidence to their rescue attempt. While Andrew listened, stunned, they described how they, and their servants, pulled Cyril from the pond and checked him.

"I–I cannot believe . . ." Andrew's voice faded. "Cyril . . . dead?"

"There was nothing we could do," Sir Chanders said, his tone kind. "Unfortunately, he was already gone."

"He must have stumbled and fell down the embankment," Lord Fornay speculated.

"It is deuced slippery out tonight, with all this rain," Sir Chanders added.

"And he was quite foxed," Edward stated, coming to stand beside Andrew and placing a hand on his shoulder.

Andrew could barely believe it. He was glad for his friend's gesture of strength as he felt all of his energy leave his body.

Cyril's celebrations had been his own undoing.

"I appreciate your trying to rescue him," Andrew said, his voice strained. "Gentlemen, come by the fire. Henry, can you get them a drink?" Henry hurried to pour them each a brandy. "Poor Cyril," Andrew continued quietly. "This is . . . quite a shock." He went to a chair and sat down abruptly.

"Especially with his father just passing on," Lord Fornay stated, seating himself too. "You have our deepest sympathies, my lord."

It was at that precise moment that Andrew realized the import of Cyril's death and Lord Fornay's words.

He had become the new Marquis of Whitbury.

Chapter Two

"Yes, daughters? You wished to speak to me?"

The Honorable Roderick Rawlings, third son of the Earl of Denton, made an imposing figure as he sat down behind the huge wood desk in his study. Weak morning sunlight entered the room through the windows, foretelling a cool spring day.

Justine swallowed, reminding herself that Father, though firm, had always been one to listen to reason. The question nagging at her was, would he think her sister's request reasonable? This might be harder than she had imagined when Charlotte first begged for her help.

Justine sat beside her sister in front of the desk and prepared to take charge of the conversation.

She sensed rather then saw Charlotte stiffen in her seat and placed a comforting hand on her sister's arm.

"We are here to talk to you about Charlotte's future," Justine said in a calm, soothing tone. As

Father raised his eyebrows, she continued, anticipating his next comment. "I am here because it affects me, in a way."

"Go on," he said.

Justine glanced at her sister. Charlotte's face was pale, and the imploring look would be hard for their father to miss.

"You know that Charlotte and Kevin have long had a great affection for each other. And Kevin is a man of upstanding character." Kevin Mayneworth, the son of a minor baron whose estates adjoined the Rawlings' sprawling country lands, had cared deeply for Charlotte since they were quite young. And Charlotte returned his feelings.

"This is true."

"And Kevin asked recently for her hand in marriage," Justine continued. She had an urge to grip her hands together, and fought it. She tried to look relaxed, hoping it would rub off on Charlotte.

There was a pause, during which the clock on the mantle seemed to tick louder than it normally did.

"He did so," Father said slowly. "And I told him that, although I had no objection to him—he is a fine young man and comes from a good family—it is not yet time for Charlotte to marry. You know this, daughters." His expression was stern.

"Some women marry at the age of seventeen," Justine said.

"Yes—Adele Pritworthy . . ." Charlotte began nervously.

Father waved his hand. "I do not want to hear of Adele Pritworthy or any others like her. Her father is a wastrel and anxious to marry off his remaining daughters. None of my daughters or sons need rush into marriage."

"And we appreciate that, Father," Justine said smoothly, giving him a smile. Often she had been thankful that her parents were not urging her to choose a husband just so they could proclaim an engagement, as was happening to some of her friends. After all, she was nineteen and entering her second season. She knew her mother, Mary, had had several suitors but waited until her second season before she and her parents had agreed upon Justine's father, Roderick, as Mary's future spouse.

But Justine had not yet met anyone she felt she could live with for the rest of her life. And she was quite relieved that her parents were not pushing her into an unwanted marriage.

Charlotte, though, was another matter. For many years she had been fond of Kevin; and now Justine knew they were truly in love.

"Charlotte is mature enough to enter marriage, I am convinced of it," Justine said, "even though she is young."

Charlotte nodded eagerly. "Mama has taught me well how to run a household—"

"Charlotte has not yet come out," Father said sharply. "You girls know it would not be proper for her to become engaged until after her coming out."

"And this is what we wanted to ask of you," Justine said.

"I want to come out a year early," Charlotte piped up hopefully.

"And I have no objection," Justine finished. Indeed, she had always been close to Charlotte, who was only two years younger than Justine. If Father wanted Charlotte to come out before the bans were read, Justine did not mind sharing a season with her. In fact, it would undoubtedly be fun to attend parties with her sister, she was certain. She was hoping Father would not object to the idea.

Father leaned forward. "Even if Charlotte came out early—and I would have to think on this and discuss it with your mother before I consented—she still could not marry Kevin just now."

In the light, Roderick's face and features looked firm as he regarded his two eldest daughters.

"But why?" asked Justine. She had agreed to lead this discussion at Charlotte's request, because Charlotte tended to be somewhat intimidated by Father. But she had held a suspicion that Father would not relent easily.

"Because you are not yet married, Justine."

Justine stared at Father, and heard Charlotte murmur in distress.

Justine had feared this objection but had not voiced it to her sister. She'd held some slight hope that their father would not hold with this particular custom, to which many families adhered.

She should have realized that their traditional father would not waver on this issue.

Father leaned forward. "The Rawlings family has always been known as one of the proudest, oldest families in England. We pride ourselves on being a proper family, law-abiding and loyal to the crown. And this means following established conventions as they should be."

Justine and her siblings had heard this lecture before. She waited, wondering what more her father would add.

Father gave a brief smile. "I am proud that my sons and daughters show signs that they, too, will uphold our fine family traditions, just as my brothers and sister and I have."

They had heard this part of the speech about fine family traditions oftentimes as well.

"But Kevin's family is a fine one, you have said so yourself," Justine reminded him.

"Yes, that is so. But the fact remains, daughter. You are older than Charlotte. Older daughters *must* marry before younger ones."

Justine's heart slowly sank, and she imagined Charlotte's was doing the same.

Charlotte made a protesting sound.

"You mean Charlotte cannot marry until I do?" Justine asked, probing in the faint hope that she was wrong.

"That is correct." Father inclined his head. "It is not proper for a younger daughter to marry before her older sister does."

Charlotte burst out, "But why, Father? Why is it not—"

"It is not *proper*," he repeated, his voice taking on a foreboding note. "This is the way things are. When one goes against conventions, tongues wag. You can be sure no one has ever been able to say anything malicious about *our* family, because we are proper."

"But I have no objection," Justine said, sending a warning glance Charlotte's way. If Charlotte resorted to emotional behavior, Father would never go along with her request. He prided himself on being a man of reason, as well as a man of propriety.

"You should have an objection," he said, leveling a look at Justine. She found herself clutching at the folds of her green gown, the smooth material bending against her fingers.

"Why is that?"

"Because if a younger daughter were to marry first, everyone would assume there was something wrong with the elder daughter. That for some reason she was unmarriageable. And then no one would want her. It happened to the elder daughter of the Earl of Satherwood. She never married. I know, because she came out the same year as my sister Emily did."

"But . . . Father!" Charlotte protested. "Justine is beautiful and intelligent; there are many men who would be glad . . ."

Father was shaking his head. "You shall not change my mind on this," he said, his tone firm as a stone walk-way. "I will not have Justine's future risked."

"But the occurrence with the earl's daughter was long ago, Father," Justine said, deliberately keeping her voice gentle and reasoning. "I believe people do not always think this way today." At least, she hoped they did not. "And I certainly have no objection to Charlotte marrying before I do. She happens to have found the right man for her, and I have not."

But their father continued to shake his head. "You will not sway me on this, daughters. Justine shall marry first, then you, Charlotte. Just as it will be when it comes time for your sisters Ginette and Arabella."

Justine and Charlotte both began talking, but Roderick held up an imperious hand.

"I believe there is nothing more to say," he said, his tone growing harder. "Charlotte, Kevin will wait for you. And Justine, you will eventually find a suitable husband, and then you shall precede Charlotte to the altar."

Justine opened her mouth to say one more thing, then closed it as she saw Father's face set in the pattern of one who had his mind firmly made up.

She knew there was no use arguing further with him this day. Perhaps, if he thought about it, he might change his mind; but further protests at this moment would simply annoy him and cause him to be less willing to hear any arguments at a later date.

Charlotte made a small sound, and Father glanced at her.

"Tears will not change my mind," he said sternly. "And your mother is in full agreement with me. She was one of seven children, as you know, and each of her sisters got married in turn. And her brothers married in birth order too, at an older age, as is proper."

"Yes, Father," Justine murmured, and nudged Charlotte's foot with her own. Better for Charlotte to seem to go along with Father now, and then approach him again when some time had passed. She smoothed the soft folds of her gown, wondering if Charlotte would be patient for a fortnight.

But before Charlotte could say anything, or not, a brisk knock came at the door.

"M'lord?" It was the formal voice of Danvers, their

butler. "I am most sorry to interrupt, but it is an urgent matter."

"Enter," Father called.

Danvers bore a sealed paper. He bowed and presented it to Father.

"This just came by courier, m'lord. He said it was most urgent, from the Marquis of Whitbury."

Father stood, eyebrows raised, and broke the seal on the note. He scanned it rapidly, and uttered a loud gasp.

"What is it?" Justine asked, sensing something disturbing had happened. Father was not easily perturbed.

He looked up, clearly shocked. "Cyril Pennington, the new Marquis of Whitbury, died last night. Drowned in the pond by Green's Gentleman's Club."

"But he just became the marquis!" exclaimed Justine. Only yesterday afternoon their father had reported the demise of the elderly marquis, Elias Pennington.

Father was well acquainted with the Pennington family, having been the closest friend of old Elias Pennington's younger brother William, until the death of William and his wife several years ago.

"Yes." Father shook his head. "This is most unusual; and most disturbing. It seems that Cyril—well, he died not even a day after his father passed on."

"He drowned?" Charlotte asked, her voice shocked too.

"The pond there is not very deep," Justine observed. They had ridden by it often enough.

"Yes, but—and this is to go no further than these walls, daughters—it seems that Cyril had been imbibing overmuch at the club. Drowning his sorrow, perhaps." Justine caught the shade of sarcasm in Father's voice.

Danvers coughed. Justine wondered if, like her, he had to swallow a chuckle. Even she had heard the gossip that Cyril couldn't wait for his father to pass on, so he could get control of the family money. She had met Cyril several times at social gatherings, and had not been impressed by his self-important ways.

Roderick took a step forward. "I must go to speak with Andrew immediately, and offer him whatever aid I can. Danvers, please order my carriage at once."

"Yes, m'lord." Danvers disappeared.

Justine had spent time with Andrew and his older sisters on many occasions, when their families had visited with the Penningtons at their estate or at the Rawlings' home. Millicent and Andrew had been quite merry; Elizabeth was quieter and more serious. But Andrew, a handsome lad, had also been a tease. Justine had been quite angered the day he dropped a worm on her best hat.

She had not seen him at parties for the ton; she supposed that, like many men his age, he had been spending some time touring the continent, then taking care of his family's estates after his parents died.

"This means that . . ." she began.

Father met her eyes.

"Yes," he said. "Andrew is the new Marquis of Whitbury."

Chapter Three

Andrew threaded his way through the crowd, scanning the room for signs of Edward or Henry or any of his other friends. He had to get out of here, and perhaps one of them would aid with his escape.

The large hall was packed with members of the ton, who had just enjoyed a delightful musicale sponsored by Baron and Lady Sandworth. The Sandworths' musical entertainments, long known as being among the finest of events, always drew a large crowd. Since the baron had been a friend of Andrew's late father, it would have been unseemly for Andrew to decline an invitation for the evening. Besides, he had known in advance that they would have truly wonderful music, as they always did. The spectacular renditions of Mozart on the pianoforte and violin had negated the onerous attention he received before the musicale began. But now, following the concluding aria by a well-known Italian singer, Andrew was anxious to avoid the matrons with marriageable daughters who had been pursuing him of late.

"Lord Whitbury!" A large matron dressed in purple suddenly blocked his way, her fat hand gripping the arm of a tall, plain daughter. "Please allow me to introduce my daughter, Penelope. She is a patron of music such as yourself." The woman gave her daughter a slight shake.

"Uh . . . um . . . my lord." The daughter stumbled over her words, then hastily curtsied.

"A pleasure, I'm sure," Andrew replied gallantly, bowing. "And Lady Foxleigh," he said, bowing to the beaming matron. "Please excuse me; it is most urgent that I speak to a friend of mine."

With a stiff smile he escaped the woman's clutches.

"Why did you not try to engage him in conversation?" the woman hissed to her daughter as Andrew hurried down the hall.

He spotted another determined mother making her way over to him, practically dragging yet another eligible female by her side. Although this one was more attractive, he was tired of having young ladies thrust at him every time he was out and about.

"Andrew! Over here!"

The voice of his friend Edward was more than welcome, and Andrew turned toward the sound with relief. He saw Edward at once, standing near the doorway, his brother Lawrence beside him.

He rapidly made his way over to the two.

"Edward, Lawrence. It is more than good to see you," Andrew said with emphasis, joining them.

"Ah yes, we couldn't help noticing the many mamas

attempting to block your way, Andrew," Edward said with a laugh. "I believe you will be declared the most eligible bachelor of the season if you don't watch out."

Andrew shuddered. "That is not what I wish." Having one young lady after another put in his path at parties was growing quite tiresome.

In truth, he had no objection to marriage. He knew he was expected someday to pick a woman who would be a good wife and companion. He hoped to have a wife who would be pleasant company, and give him children. But he hadn't expected to be a marquis, nor his wife a marchioness—and he hadn't expected someday to turn into Right Now.

Not, of course, that he was obligated to marry immediately. But, as his sisters pointed out a mere month ago, following his uncle's and cousin's funerals, it was now more important than ever that he have an heir.

He knew his parents had approved suitable husbands for Millicent and Elizabeth. But his parents had taken into account his sisters' wishes and chosen husbands of whom the girls were fond. They had, likewise, always expected Andrew to choose a suitable wife for whom he held some affection.

"We shall all marry eventually, my friend," Edward said. "But it seems you are fated to marry sooner than the rest of us."

"There is no rush," Andrew pointed out. "I am only twenty-five."

"Ah, but you are now a marquis," Lawrence said. "And considered a prime bachelor."

"It rather sounds like I am a cut of meat," Andrew said dryly.

Edward laughed. "It does, doesn't it? In the marriage mart, I suppose all gentlemen and ladies are no more than goods, with some more prime than others." He dropped his voice, his eyes gleaming. "Take Lady Driscoll, for instance. Now there's a prime example of—"

"Lord Whitbury!"

Andrew grimaced at the sound of yet another female voice.

"Lord Whitbury." The tone became imploring. A hand touched his arm, a little too heavily.

He turned to face Isobel Newmont.

Isobel, his late cousin's intended, was an attractive but haughty woman with pale blond hair and blue-gray eyes. A tall woman, she was nevertheless quite striking in appearance. That is, if you had a penchant for faces that were classically beautiful but stone cold. Her late father, who had passed on some four or five years prior, had been the fourth son of an earl. And Isobel's late mother had been most anxious for her to wed a titled gentlemen, Andrew had heard. Isobel's mother had been ecstatic when Isobel became engaged to Cyril, since he was slated to inherit the title of Marquis of Whitbury; almost immediately after the engagement was announced, Mrs. Newmont had succumbed to heart failure and passed away. They said that on her deathbed she had declared her job done, to betroth her only daughter to a man with a title.

Isobel stood now, with her brother Darren behind her, her usually unemotional face wearing a saddened expression.

"Lord Whitbury," she repeated, "I am so glad to see you here this night. Please have a word with me regarding your cousin, Cyril." She accompanied her words with an audible sniffle.

"Certainly." Andrew knew the reluctance was evident in his voice. But how could he refuse?

Isobel was dressed in palest blue tonight, a color that reflected her eyes. As he stepped aside with her, she took a handkerchief from her reticule and dabbed at her eyes. Andrew saw no tears there. But her strong floral perfume was cloying, and he coughed.

"Yes?" he asked, wanting to get straight to the point.

"I am beside myself." Isobel put a hand dramatically to her chest, yet her voice remained totally impassive.

"Oh?"

"Since Cyril's untimely death"—she closed her eyes briefly, then reopened them—"since his passing, I . . . dear me!" She swayed, and Andrew was forced to reach out and take hold of her elbow.

She cast him a glance that, he thought, was meant to be appealing.

But he found himself quite unmoved by the performance.

He had never thought for an instant that Isobel cared for his cousin; no, with her background, it seemed obvious that she was marrying Cyril for his title—and money.

Not that this was an unusual occurrence among polite British society. In fact, it was commonplace. And, he had no illusions about his own position. He knew many young ladies and their families found him highly eligible because of his newly acquired title; the fact that he was wealthy, considered handsome and pleasant, was a plus.

"Thank you, my lord," Isobel was murmuring. She looked up at him again. Observing that she appeared quite steady on her feet, Andrew released her elbow.

"I am quite beside myself," Isobel repeated. "Cyril meant so much to me, you know. His sudden death—I just don't know what I shall do."

Andrew tried to come up with some consoling words. "We were all quite shocked by his untimely passing."

"Yes." Isobel almost pounced on the words. "That is it exactly, my lord. I am so glad you understand." She paused, giving her brother Darren, who had sidled up to her left, a quick look.

Darren chimed in. "Yes, my sister has been inconsolable these past weeks," he said woodenly.

Andrew wondered if perhaps he was witnessing a practiced scene. The words were pat and dry, unemotional. He looked beyond Isobel and saw Edward and Lawrence, only a few feet away, grinning at him.

"Of course," he said.

"I have been quite . . . quite"—Isobel paused—"inconsolable, as Darren has said."

"I do understand. Now, if you'll excuse me, I must finish—"

"You do understand, my lord," she said hastily. "Cyril's death has been so tragic, such a great loss for me."

I'm sure, Andrew thought sardonically.

"It would be such a great comfort," Isobel continued, drawing closer, "if you would come by my home soon and visit with me. It would be so very consoling to spend time with someone who also mourns Cyril's passing." Her voice, hushed, grew more intense, and she sent Andrew another imploring look.

Andrew swallowed uncomfortably. He had no desire to spend time consoling Isobel. If that was indeed all she wanted.

"Perhaps I can visit at a later date," he hedged, starting to move away. "I have so many duties to perform, you understand. My uncle's estates—"

"Yes, yes," Isobel said, somewhat impatiently. She stopped, as if realizing her impatience was showing. "I know you must have a large amount of work before you, my lord, what with the marquis' and Cyril's untimely deaths." She paused and Andrew wondered if she was trying to recall a scripted scene she had planned. "But if you could spare me but a brief amount of your time . . ." Another look. Then she smiled, although it didn't reach her eyes. "I have been so grieved. Even a short visit from you, another who mourns Cyril, would be most welcome."

Andrew was certain now she was acting out a rehearsed speech. It would be rude to refuse, and yet he had absolutely no desire to spend even the tiniest amount of time with this cold, calculating woman.

Isobel, with her scheming nature, might even try to trap him into matrimony.

"Well, perhaps in a week or two," Andrew replied, deliberately sounding vague. "I do have to check on our estates to the north; and I have many things yet to go over with my man of business . . . I will see what I can do." He gave Isobel a stiff smile, and a quick bow. "And now I must be off. I do hope you find some consolation in attending such events as tonight's musicale."

"I . . ." Isobel began, but Andrew was already moving away. "Thank you, my lord," she said hastily. "I shall look forward to your visit." She curtsied quickly.

Andrew escaped, hurrying down the hall. He noted Edward's laughing expression.

Well, let him entertain Isobel.

Even as Andrew thought the words, he noticed Edward turning to his brother and pulling him in another direction, away from Cyril's intended.

Andrew scolded himself, realizing he must become more adept at these quick leave-takings. He opened a door that led to the terrace and quickly slid through.

Incidents such as these were increasing in frequency. He would have to do even better in the future, he concluded.

The rooms at Sandworth Manor were overcrowded and becoming stuffy. Following the conclusion of the musical entertainment, Justine went in search of some fresh air, leaving her parents engaged in a jovial conversation with Baron and Lady Sandworth.

Ducking down a side hall, Justine successfully avoided a duke's son who was incredibly boring. Since she had visited the manor often with her family, she knew several ways to get to the lovely terrace. Within moments she had found the small blue parlor and, opening the French doors, slipped out into the evening.

She paused, breathing deeply of the cooler night air. Although the early May evening was unusually warm, compared to the air inside the crowded manor, the air outside was deliciously refreshing. Flowers scented the soft air.

She moved out onto the terrace, which overlooked Baron and Lady Sandworth's lavish gardens, breathing in a floral scent she was unable to recognize. Noise from the house was subdued here, but as her eyes adjusted to the dark, lit by only a few candles in strategic corners, she caught a glimpse of a couple hurrying down the stone steps to the garden.

A secret tryst? She wondered, and smiled. How romantic!

She looked up at the sky. A partial moon peeked out from scurrying clouds. Breathing deeply, she let the night air envelope her. And tried not to feel envy for the young lovers she had seen.

What would it be like? she wondered as she walked toward the stone balustrade, to have a man pull you into the garden like that? Perhaps kiss you and declare his undying love?

It would be blissful, she thought, leaning out to look over the gardens where the two had disappeared. But, unlikely to happen.

Justine was practical enough to know that when she became engaged, it would be to someone who her family thought would be a good match for her. Not that her parents would ever force her to marry someone she abhorred—they had made it clear she was to find someone she actually *liked*, who would make a proper husband.

"My parents and I knew your father would be a good match for me," Justine's mother, Mary, had told her often enough. "His father was an earl and mine was a duke. We both came from old, esteemed, wealthy families. But your father and I were fond of each other, and we enjoyed each other's company. We also shared similar views on many topics. It was an ideal match."

"But what about love?" Justine had asked her mother, curious.

Her mother had smiled. "Love grows as you spend time with your husband. The same will happen to you, I'm sure."

Justine had wondered at her mother's words. Yes, Mary and Roderick did seem to care for each other. But wouldn't it be wonderful to actually fall in love with someone and then marry him? That's the way it happened in the novels she was so fond of reading. She gazed out into the gardens again, listening for the young couple.

"Falling in love is not what usually happens in life," her mother had declared many times. "One must be sensible, Justine."

Even her friends were warning her against her romantic notions. One after another had married suitable husbands of whom their parents had approved, sometimes without their own liking. Justine had run into one particular friend here at the musicale and the poor girl looked miserable beside her pompous, older husband.

Except, of course, for Priscilla, an old friend. Priscilla had shocked the ton at the end of last season when she had run off to Gretna Green and eloped with a sea captain she had met the year before on a trip to Europe. Justine wondered how Priscilla was now.

Of course, she knew there were happy endings for some girls—finding a man you loved who was also suitable. After all, her sister Charlotte was in love with Kevin, and her parents felt this would eventually be a good match.

Was it too much to hope that the same would happen to her?

Justine lifted her face to the moon, letting the cool air touch her heated skin. She breathed deeply, smelling again the sweet flowery scent. Stars twinkled in the sky, almost seeming to wink at her. She thought she heard a whisper in the garden, quickly hushed. She fingered her seed pearl pin, the one given to her by her mother when she turned sixteen. The pearls felt smooth and cool, and she knew they almost glowed against her gown, a jewel-blue color.

Then she heard a sound nearby and glanced over her shoulder, in time to see a man slip through another pair of French doors at the end of the terrace, and move over to where she stood in the shadows.

He came closer, and a cloud blocked the moon's rays. He hesitated, apparently waiting until his eyes adjusted to the darkness. After a few seconds, he moved forward.

He was tall, and slim, and carried himself well. As he approached, the moon reappeared and Justine got a look at his face.

She recognized him at once. It was Andrew Pennington, the new Marquis of Whitbury.

It had been nearly five years since she had seen him. Father had told them that Andrew had been traveling on the continent, and then spending time taking care of family business after his parents' tragic deaths in a carriage accident. During Justine's first season, he had not been in London at all.

Now, with the moon coming out from behind the clouds, she could see his face quite clearly—and she caught her breath.

When, she wondered, had Andrew become so handsome? Well, perhaps he had been so when she was a girl of fourteen, and he a young man of twenty, when last they saw each other at his parents' garden party. But she couldn't remember him looking anything but mischievous that day. In fact, she recalled that he had taken a ribbon from her hair and she and Charlotte had gone dashing after him.

But where his face had been that of a young man's when last she saw it, it was now the face of a man grown.

A very handsome gentleman.

His dark blond hair curled around his striking face. Eyes she knew, a pure, deep blue, surveyed the terrace as he walked. His nose was straight, and his chin strong. His broad shoulders were encased in a well-tailored jacket that seemed to be crimson in color.

He stopped a yard from her, apparently seeing for the first time that someone else occupied the terrace "I beg your pardon, my lady," he said formally. "I had no idea someone was in this corner. The shadows make it difficult to see."

"There is no need to be so formal with me, Andrew," she said, addressing him by his given name instead of by his title.

A puzzled look creased his face. "Do I know you, my lady?"

She stepped closer, so that she stood nearer to the candles as the moon scooted beneath clouds again. He stared at her, and she realized that although she knew him, he did not recognize her.

"You don't know me, do you?" she asked, a smile tugging at her mouth. For once she had something to tease Andrew about.

"No, but I would be happy to remedy that," he replied gallantly, studying her face.

"Does the tale of a worm dropped on a hat bring about recollections?" Justine asked somewhat tartly.

"A worm on a—*Justine*?" An incredulous expression spread over his face.

"The very one," Justine said, and dipped into a curtsy. "My lord. I was so sorry to learn about your uncle's demise, and that of your cousin, Cyril. I wanted to attend the funeral, but Father insisted it was an occasion for him and Mother only to attend."

"That's quite all right. No need for you to be so formal, either. We are old friends, indeed. But—Justine! I did not recognize you. You have . . . grown, haven't you?"

The way he said her given name—with such surprise, almost delight—sent a shimmer along her spine. She barely had time to wonder why. "Yes, I suppose I have grown."

He grabbed her hands in his large, warm ones. "My word, look at you! You're all grown up. You're—" He swiftly dropped her hands, and bowed. "You are a young woman," he said solemnly. "When last I saw you, you must have been only ten or so."

"Fourteen," Justine corrected, her hands tingling

strangely from his touch. "That was five years ago." She hoped she looked mature, but right now the unfamiliar sensations whirling inside of her were causing her to feel like a young girl again.

"Fourteen," he murmured, his eyes still fastened on hers. "And you . . . you have come out, I take it?"

"Last year," she murmured.

"Ah, yes. I remember now, I was invited to the ball at Rawlings Manor, however I was detained at one of our estates up near Bradford. How are you, and your parents? Perhaps I will see them here?"

"We are fine," Justine said, finding it easier to speak of her family than of herself. She let out a slight breath. "Yes, my parents are here for the musicale."

"Your father has been a big help to me," Andrew said, his voice solemn. "Since I had to assume responsibility so . . . suddenly. And your sisters and brothers? They are well too?"

"All well. Charlotte is here in London and will come out next year. Walter is away at school, and George will follow in two years. He is also in London now. And Ginette and Arabella are still in the schoolroom."

"Of course," he said, still staring at her. Justine leaned against the stone balustrade, feeling somewhat awkward under Andrew's intent gaze. Her heart was beating noticeably faster than usual. "I was very sorry to hear about the deaths in your family," she repeated quietly. "It must have been quite a shock when Cyril passed away so soon after your Uncle Elias."

"Quite a shock," he said dryly. "Not Uncle—he had hung on to life for many years, despite his declining health. Yet he had continued to supervise all his business ventures. But that morning he had a number of spells, and the doctor summoned me. I was able to see him just before he passed on." Andrew turned and gazed out over the dark gardens. His voice took on a stringent note. "Cyril, though, that is quite a different story."

If Justine had not known Andrew and his family for many years, she might have hesitated to speak about the subject further. But she guessed it would not offend Andrew.

"I know that Cyril drowned in the pond near your club," she said softly. "My father told us about your note."

"It is true." Andrew sighed. "It is commonly known that he had gotten totally foxed before he left the club. I myself offered to take him home, since he was so unsteady on his feet. But Cyril refused."

"From my understanding, that has happened before," Justine said, keeping her tone gentle. She turned to stare at the gardens along with Andrew. "But of course, Father does not like to discuss such matters with his daughters. He did not give us many details."

"Yes . . . Roderick is much like my own father was."

"I know he misses your father to this day," Justine added softly. "They were the best of friends."

"Like myself and my friend Edward."

There was a lull, and Justine sought something to say.

"How," she began cautiously, "do you feel about becoming a marquis?"

"How do I feel?" Andrew ran a hand through his hair, and gave a short laugh. "That's funny. I often have contradictory feelings. The shock of inheriting the title has not yet worn off. I had to quickly become acquainted with Uncle Elias' business dealings and the Whitbury land holdings. I barely had time to think about it. Sometimes I am grateful that it fell into my hands. I used to fear that Cyril would . . . well, ignore the estates and go through all of Uncle's money." He stopped, lowering his voice. "This is between us, Justine." He turned to regard her, his expression serious. "I would not have that repeated."

"You know you can trust me. I shan't repeat this to anyone. I know your family, after all, for many years." She paused. "You were saying, your feelings were mixed?"

"Yes. Other times, I find the attention I am garnering now as a marquis can be very annoying." He grinned suddenly, and Justine could see the face of the boy he had been. "Especially at social functions such as this one. The only reason I came was because I knew the music would be outstanding and because Baron and Lady Sandworth are family friends."

"I imagine you are garnering a large amount of attention, as you say," she said, smiling too. "People want to become fast friends with the new marquis."

"The men do. Men who barely recognized me before are now asking my opinion on all sorts of matters. And the women—" He stopped, and grimaced. From out in the garden Justine heard a giggle, quickly smothered.

Andrew raised his brows.

"There is a couple in the garden," whispered Justine. "Please continue."

"I see. Well, the women are . . . well, I suppose chasing me about sums it up. The more daring of the young women are making eyes at me, and the mothers are thrusting the shyer ones in my path every chance they get." He laughed, but with little amusement. "I am beginning to feel that I am rather a commodity."

"Ah . . ." Justine said. "But don't you like having all of London's most eligible young ladies at your feet?" As she said the words, a curious feeling gripped her. A feeling of . . . consternation. The idea of dozens of women pursuing Andrew was curiously distasteful.

"No. Not that I don't plan to marry someday, but . . . for the moment, I would like to be left alone."

"That is unlikely to happen."

"True." He sighed heavily. The sound seemed to linger in the quiet, moonlit garden.

The young couple at the outskirts of the garden was silent now. The moon was again casting light on the terrace, and somewhere close by an owl hooted suddenly. Justine started.

"I wish there was some way to keep these mamas and young women from chasing me," Andrew said thoughtfully. "It has been happening for only a few weeks, and already it is tiresome, to say the least."

"There really is no way to stop the pursuit. It will keep happening until you select a wife."

Andrew sighed again. "I suppose so. I will have to learn to be harsher in avoiding encounters with eligible ladies." He gazed at her, and once again Justine felt she was being studied. Self-conscious, she turned to look out at the garden once more. What did he think of her after five years?

"I suppose you could escape into the garden for a while, and hide."

"I was doing that when I saw you," Andrew told her,

chuckling. "But I am delighted to see you. Eventually, though, I shall have to go back and brave the crowd in the house, even if it is only for a brief good-bye to our host and hostess."

"You will survive, I'm sure," she said, smiling.

The main door to the terrace opened suddenly, and a merry group came out. Some of the gentlemen and ladies were laughing, and one young man was singing off-key.

"Quick," Andrew said, grabbing Justine's hand. "Let's make our getaway!" And he pulled her down the stone steps.

"But—" Justine protested. She hurried to keep up with Andrew's long legs. She kept her voice hushed, not wanting anyone to recognize them. What would people think if they saw her dashing into the deeper shadows with the new marquis?

They'd think we were secret sweethearts. Just like that first couple.

They had reached the tall bushes, and Andrew drew her along, until they blended into the midnight darkness.

As soon as they were behind a tall bush, she tried to stop, and Andrew ceased pulling her.

"What will people think if we are seen?" she hissed.

He grinned. "We are out for a late night stroll. Don't worry, Justine. If anyone sees us, I will assure them that as a family friend, I am simply looking out for your welfare."

Why was that idea so disappointing, she wondered, while the thought of being in the garden late at night, alone with Andrew, as if they were sweethearts, was an exciting one?

"Come, my dear," Andrew said in a gallant voice, "I shall protect you from any gentlemen who would make unseemly overtures. Let's stroll along the path." As he spoke, he tucked her hand into the crook of his arm and started forward.

"Thank you, gallant sir," Justine said, trying to match his jovial tone. But inside her heart was beating rapidly, and she had grown quite warm.

It couldn't be Andrew who was making her feel this way, could it? Andrew, the young man who had teased and tormented her and her sisters. It must be the midnight air, the moon skidding in and out of the clouds, the clandestine atmosphere of being in the garden alone with him, that was making her feel almost giddy.

But she had walked in romantic gardens before in the company of other men. And not one of them had ever made her heart beat faster.

It was the first time she had ever felt *romantic* about it, she realized.

The scent of lilacs drifted to meet them as they began to walk along the stone walkway. Justine tried to breathe slowly, waiting for the excitement she was feeling to diminish.

But all she could feel was a heightened awareness as she walked beside Andrew. Every little sound—an insect buzzing, the owl hooting again—seemed louder than normal. The floral scents were especially pleasing, and the moon, weaving in and out of the clouds, cast long, atmospheric shadows around them. The night air seemed to sparkle. It was as if the whole garden was bewitched.

Andrew felt Justine's hand tighten on his arm. He

stole another look at her as they moved silently through the dark garden.

He had not recognized Justine Rawlings when he first came upon her. She had grown from a cute girl with a cherubic face into a stunningly lovely young woman. Her features were perfect, framed by dark hair. It was too dark to see the color of her eyes, but he thought they were a deep brown. Her mouth was lovely, and when she smiled, her face looked enchanting.

It was hard to keep his eyes off her. She was beautiful, and must have her share of suitors. She seemed to be as intelligent and personable as he remembered.

So what was so fascinating about Justine that he felt compelled to pull her into the garden instead of leaving the party? Was it merely because he wanted to catch up with an old family friend? Or avoid the crowd that had come out onto the terrace? Or because he enjoyed being in the company of an attractive woman who was capable of both witty conversation and talking about heartfelt matters like his family circumstances?

That must be it, he decided. Justine was someone he felt he could easily talk to. That was why he was spending time here in the shadows with her.

It had nothing to do, of course, with the fact that he was amazed to see that she had grown into a lovely young woman. Nothing to do with the fact that, at this very moment, he was tempted to gaze into her eyes.

The night air must be affecting him, he thought, shaking his head slightly. Where in heavens had that last thought come from?

Too little sleep during the last several weeks, plus dealing with new Whitbury estate burdens on top of his own Pennington estates, and two funerals, must be making him light-headed. He should really head for home and get a good night's rest.

But as he walked beside Justine, he felt curiously content, and unwilling to break the comfortable bond they were sharing.

A smile touched Justine's mouth as they heard another giggle not too far away. "It is so lovely out here," Justine said, her voice soft. "It's no wonder we are not the only couple enjoying the evening air."

"Perhaps someone is having a clandestine meeting," Andrew said, tilting his head towards the section of the garden from whence the sounds emanated. "Spies or the like."

"You always liked imagining adventures," Justine accused, but her voice was lilting. "I remember one time, visiting your family, when you convinced my brothers to play pirates with you." She paused and shook her head, a smile on her face. "Now, I think there are two sweethearts hiding in the garden, meeting secretly, before they must go back to the party. Perhaps their parents come from feuding families—"

Andrew laughed quietly. "You must keep your head in the same romantic books that my sisters Millicent and Elizabeth like to read."

"I do like to read. I am not ashamed of it."

"Are you a veritable bluestocking then? Always quoting from Shakespeare and Aristotle?"

"Why is it that if a man studies these things, he is regarded as well educated; but if a woman does, she is referred to as a bluestocking?"

"I don't know." Andrew shrugged. "Well, are you a bluestocking?"

"I am only considered an avid reader, no more. Bluestockings always have their noses in books. I also enjoy music and parties and most of the things ladies my age like."

"Such as . . . handsome suitors?" Andrew said, making his voice mocking.

"Only if they are intelligent and polite. And are not terrible teases."

Andrew laughed out loud. He couldn't help it.

"Shh." Justine paused and jostled his arm. "I do have a reputation to maintain."

"Meaning you should not be caught in a dark garden with a family friend who is laughing at your quips?" Andrew knew what she meant. A short stroll in the garden with a family friend her parents knew might be considered innocent if they returned promptly; too long an absence, or too much merriment, might cause raised eyebrows. And despite his teasing, he respected Justine and her family too much to want to cause any undue gossip.

"Just so," she said.

"Then we shall turn around." Andrew steered her back in the direction they'd come from. "But I do so with great reluctance. We must continue this spirited conversation another time."

He meant what he said. As they walked down the path, he found himself smiling. It had been quite a while since he'd enjoyed himself this way. At least four weeks. Since Elias' and Cyril's deaths, it seemed he had not paused to smile.

"I look forward to it," Justine was saying.

"Then I will return you to your father, and give him my regards. He was a great help to me in dealing with the two funerals. I will ask if I can call upon your family soon so we may continue this conversation at a later date."

They moved out of the deeply shadowed section of the garden into the moonlit area near the terrace. Justine dropped her hand and took a step away, maintaining a more respectable distance from his person.

The merrymaking group on the terrace barely paid heed to them, except for Lawrence. He raised a glass to Andrew, then bent towards a red-haired young lady, who was laughing loudly.

They passed the group and entered the manor through a back hallway. The crowd was thick, and Andrew saw several people turn to stare at them.

One was the matron in the loud purple gown, and she wore a frown on her chubby face as she surveyed them.

Perhaps Justine was right. Not wanting even the smallest spot to stain her sterling reputation, he said loudly, "I am so glad to hear your family is well. I must greet your father . . . you said he's over this way?" He paused, indicating a corridor to the right.

Out of the corner of his eye he witnessed the purple-clad mama grabbing at her daughter.

Wanting to avoid her, Andrew turned to the right.

"My lord!" A short, squat young lady practically barred his way. "How good to see you!" She curtsied, then batted her lashes at him. Andrew gave a brief, required bow. As he straightened, he caught her casting a malicious look at Justine.

He knew he had met the young woman at some point, but had no recollection of her name.

Justine stepped closer. "Hello, Lady Agatha," she said smoothly, in a cool, sophisticated voice.

Agatha's jealous expression was almost comical. Andrew had to fight the desire to laugh. "Excuse us, Lady Agatha, I am looking for Roderick Rawlings."

"I believe he's over there," Justine said, waving her hand at a group in the main hall.

Successfully sidestepping Agatha, Andrew maneuvered down the hall beside Justine to where he could now see the Rawlings.

If one more young lady or mama got in his way . . . well, he wasn't sure what he would do. Grind his teeth. Push aside someone. Laugh, perhaps.

He recalled Justine's words: *There really is no way to stop the pursuit. It will keep happening until you select a wife.*

He suspected that Justine was correct.

Within the hour the Rawlings stepped out of their coach at their fashionable London residence. Once inside, Justine kissed her parents good night and moved up the curved stairway to her room.

Despite the late hour, she was wide awake. She felt like humming, only she didn't want to wake anyone.

She had enjoyed this party more than she had enjoyed any other this season.

Was it because she had spent time with Andrew?

During the ride home, she had silently debated whether to rouse Charlotte and tell her about the evening. Charlotte often stayed awake late, demanding to know the details of the parties she was eager to attend. And this time, Justine had more to talk about.

On the other hand, the unfamiliar sensations she had experienced were ones she wanted to savor, perhaps to relive privately before sharing.

By the time she reached the upper hallway and was heading to the rooms the older Rawlings children occupied, she had decided to talk to Charlotte. This rather delicious experience in an enchanting garden setting should be discussed.

Justine rapped softly on Charlotte's door. After a moment, with no answer, she knocked again.

There was still no answer. Was her sister perhaps deeply asleep? She turned the knob and slid into the room.

"Charlotte?" she whispered.

A candle burned, revealing the bed was unmade.

Where is Charlotte?

A sudden fear clutched at Justine. Charlotte had confided only last week that several nights before, she had sneaked downstairs and met Kevin alone in the garden for a midnight tryst.

Justine had chastised her, of course, and Charlotte had said she wouldn't do that again.

Could she have broken her word and crept out to meet Kevin?

If so, her sister was foolishly risking her reputation. She must find her and put a stop to this nonsense before their parents discovered what Charlotte was about.

Justine went to open the door, and stopped, hearing her parents coming up the stairs. She waited, listening intently as they moved down the opposite wing towards their chambers at the far end.

She continued to wait until after she heard the door shut. It would be several minutes until her mother's maid helped her disrobe and left the suite, so this was her chance to hurry downstairs and see if she could find Charlotte.

Justine left the room, moving swiftly, and walked down the stairs, her soft slippers making no noise. If she was stopped, she decided, she would say she was heading to the library to get something to read, for she was too awake to sleep immediately. No one would question that, as it had happened before.

She stopped by the library door. A small candle burned in the hall, casting a mild yellow glow. The lower floor of the house was silent.

Taking a deep breath, Justine walked to the end of the hall that housed the library, Father's study, and another small parlor. At the end was one door to the gardens and she opened it slowly, not wanting to make any noise.

The May evening had grown cooler, and she shivered slightly as she moved down the path to the center of the gardens, where she knew Charlotte had met Kevin previously. There was a small copse with a statue, very pretty and picturesque in the moonlight, Charlotte had declared.

"You shouldn't be there in the moonlight!" Justine had reprimanded Charlotte sternly.

As she drew close, she heard a muffled sound, followed by a whisper.

"Charlotte?" Justine hissed, keeping her voice low.

For a moment there was silence. Even the insects seemed to be asleep. "Charlotte," Justine repeated, raising her voice a notch.

"Justine?" Charlotte asked, her voice also pitched low.

Justine rounded the corner into the garden square. Charlotte stood nearby Kevin, not touching him.

But her disheveled hair and quick, audible breaths made Justine certain that only moments ago, she must have been in Kevin's arms.

Kevin was, rather ridiculously, bowing to Justine. In the moonlight she could see his face was flushed.

"Justine." He too kept his voice low.

"You are home early. How did you know where I was?" Charlotte whispered.

"Charlotte! Get inside before Mother and Father realize you are out here!" Justine said, grabbing hold of her sister's arm and giving her a little shove. "Quickly! It's later than you think. Get into the library and I will meet you there." She turned toward Kevin. "She must go, now!"

Charlotte gave Kevin a dreamy look, before picking up her skirts and hurrying down the path.

Justine frowned at Kevin. "I had thought better of you, Kevin. You should not be arranging late night trysts with my sister!"

Kevin was nodding his head. "You are right, of course, Justine. But Charlotte—"

"But Charlotte?" Justine prompted, a feeling of dread settling inside her.

"I do not want to say anything against my fiancée," he replied gallantly.

"But Charlotte asked you to meet?"

He hesitated. "Yes. She said we needed to meet, urgently."

"I will speak to her at once. I must get back before we both get into trouble. Now go, before someone sees you!" Justine hurried back up the path, and heard Kevin moving the opposite way. The path led to the back of the property, where there was a gate. Charlotte must have unlocked it.

Justine almost ran back to the house, then stopped, and slid open the door slowly. Closing it quietly, she walked to the library and entered, closing the door behind her. She paused to catch her breath.

Charlotte sat in the dark, on a sofa, waiting for her.

Moonlight peeked through the windows, enough for Justine to see Charlotte's expression. She looked both worried and determined at the same time.

"Charlotte! You told me there would be no more meetings in the garden!" Justine said, raising her voice as much as she dared. A thought had occurred to her. Maybe Charlotte hoped that if she and Kevin were caught, their parents would force them to marry?

"Charlotte," she said in her sternest voice, "if Mother and Father find you are having these . . . clandestine meetings, they will forbid you to ever marry Kevin!"

Charlotte's face became defiant. "They will not let me marry him anyway! We have tried. I cannot force you to marry before I do, Justine—and I wouldn't want you to marry without love in any case."

"Then you will simply have to wait," Justine said, her voice becoming strident. "It is not as if you will never marry Kevin; Father and Mother do like him. You will have to be patient. I'm sure I will marry someday."

"But not soon enough!" Charlotte declared dramatically. "I want so to marry Kevin and he wants to marry me. But Father won't relent, I'm convinced. I tried to talk to him while you were preparing for the musicale, and he would not listen. I think—" She sniffled loudly.

"What is it?" Justine asked. A sense of cold foreboding settled within her.

"I think Kevin and I are going to have to—run away!"

"Run away? What do you mean? You can't—"

"Yes, we can. We don't see why we should wait any longer. I am old enough. I think we are going to have to elope to Gretna Green!"

Chapter Four

Justine's mouth fell open. "Gretna Green?"

She knew, of course, of the infamous Gretna Green; eloping couples always fled there. Such as Priscilla and her sea captain. But Justine had never imagined in her wildest dreams that her sister would consider such an action.

She grabbed Charlotte's hand. "We must discuss this upstairs! Come. If anyone sees us, pretend we are talking about the musicale."

Justine pulled Charlotte into the hall, closing the library door behind them. A quick glance showed her no one was about. Only a few candles burned as they made their way down the hall and up the stairs.

Justine's heart was thumping, and the whole time her mind kept repeating, *Gretna Green! Gretna Green!*

She held her breath at the top of the stairs. All was silent.

By the time she reached Charlotte's room and practically thrust her sister inside, her stomach was tight with knots.

She glared at her sister, putting her thoughts into words. "Charlotte, how can you consider such an action?"

"Because we want to marry," Charlotte stated, sitting on the edge of her bed. "I know I love Kevin, and he loves me. He has pledged his undying devotion to me. We want to . . . be together . . . for all time." She sniffled. "Why should we wait because of Father's silly edict?"

"But–but you have not come out yet. Don't you want to?" asked Justine, grasping at whatever arguments she could. Next she would bring up the possible stain on the family name if Charlotte acted so rashly.

"There is no need," Charlotte said, shaking her head. "I want to become Kevin's wife more than anything. After we are married, there will be time enough for parties and other events. I shall go as Kevin's wife," she finished proudly.

"You will be ostracized if you elope," Justine pointed out, her tone sharp, "and invited to few places."

"Oh." Charlotte paused, and Justine knew her optimistic sister had not considered all the angles and consequences of this rash action.

"And have you considered how this will stain our family name?" Justine pressed the slight advantage she imagined she was gaining. "And Kevin's family too?"

Charlotte shook her head. "No."

"Which means it will be harder for Ginette and Arabella when it is their turn to come out, and find husbands!"

"Ginette is only ten and Arabella seven! By the time they come out, people will have forgotten."

Justine began to pace. Returning to Charlotte, she sat back down. "What about me?" she asked quietly, regarding her sister.

Charlotte stared at Justine for a minute, and Justine knew Charlotte had not considered this either.

"This will make it more difficult for me to wed," Justine said, trying to sound eminently practical. "What if I find a man whom I love, and he cares for me . . . but because of your rash actions his family does not want us to marry?"

"Well . . ." Charlotte shifted her position slightly. Then a gleam came into her eyes. "You could always elope to Gretna Green too."

Justine could not help laughing, even though she knew she shouldn't. Charlotte responded with a smile, and Justine hugged her.

"Why can you not wait until I marry?" Justine asked her sister quietly.

"That could be a long time from now."

Justine winced at Charlotte's words. "Thank you," she said dryly, not bothering to hide the sarcasm in her tone.

"Oh, I don't mean there is anything wrong with you! I mean . . . you haven't met anyone who makes your heart sing, Justine. And I know you will not marry until you do."

Was this true? Justine wondered. She had never put it into such words with her sister, but . . .

Without volition, her mind flashed back to the memory of Andrew standing in the moonlight, grabbing her hand and leading her into the garden.

And her heart gave a little skip.

She inhaled sharply, and turned to look her sister straight in the face once again. Andrew didn't make her heart sing, she thought. If anything, he could be most annoying.

Although, this evening he had been gallant.

She must focus on her sister. "Charlotte, why have you thought of eloping right now? You seemed fine with waiting just a few days ago." She tried to sweep the picture of Andrew to the back of her mind.

"We were talking and . . ." Charlotte paused. Her cheeks grew pink. "He kissed me and—"

"He kissed you?" Justine tried to sound shocked. But instead she found herself most curious about the experience. What was it like?

"Yes, and"—Charlotte paused again—"we . . . we decided we did not want to wait. We want to marry soon. After all," she said, her voice becoming more heated, "we already know we want to marry each other—why should we wait until you marry? Our minds will not change."

Justine was certain that was true. Still . . .

"You should not be kissing, Charlotte," she reproved, knowing she sounded like an elder sister. "And if you had been caught in the gardens with him . . ."

"Then perhaps Father would want us to marry straight away," Charlotte mused, biting her lip.

This would *not* do at all. Somehow Justine must convince her starry-eyed sister that elopement and midnight assignations were not the way to handle this problem.

"Charlotte," she began, placing her hand on her sister's arm, "listen to me, please. Eloping would be a mistake. Imagine how Mother and Father would feel, for one thing, and the effects on all of us."

Charlotte hesitated, and Justine began to believe she was making some progress.

"You must think of others," she said, making her voice kind. "And Kevin and his family too."

"I will think about them," Charlotte said, but she sounded uncertain.

"And I am glad to give you any help I can! But, Charlotte, you must give me a little time. I need to try to figure out how to approach Father, and what to do about your problem."

Charlotte blanched. "You will not tell him what I said about Gretna Green?"

"No, no, of course not. If you promise not to do anything rash and run away. Somehow, there must be a way to convince him to let you marry soon." Justine gazed at the single flickering candle flame which cast shadows about Charlotte's bedroom. But what would convince him? How could she persuade Father to change his mind before Charlotte went and did something foolish?

"Do you really think so?" Charlotte clutched at her skirts, hope lighting her eyes.

"Yes, I do. But give me a day or two to consider some different possibilities. If Father agrees to let you wed fairly soon, you will not run away?"

"No, of course not."

"And you will not run away while I try to come up with a plan?" Desperately, Justine wondered how on earth she could convince her father to let Charlotte marry before she did.

"No."

"Then I will try to figure something out." Justine patted Charlotte's hand. All the while, her mind was racing. What? How? She wished she could be as confident as she sounded to her younger sister. But at least she had stalled Charlotte's insane plan.

"Oh, thank you, Justine." Charlotte threw her arms around her and hugged her tightly. "I know you will help."

But as Justine left the room, she wondered how on earth she could solve Charlotte's problem.

Sleep eluded Justine for some time. Thoughts of Charlotte disturbed her, and she could not immediately think of a way to convince Father to let Charlotte be the first to wed.

After a while her thoughts drifted to Andrew. Despite his rather mischievous nature, he had been charming this evening. Much to her surprise, she had enjoyed his company.

When she did fall asleep, it was to dream of Andrew—his smile, the light dancing in his eyes, and the warmth of his hand as he pulled her into the garden.

She woke later than usual, and hurried downstairs. She was the last to eat breakfast. Afterward she went outside and strolled in the garden, her thoughts tumbling. How could she avert Charlotte's actions? What should she do? Steering her mind away from memories of her encounter with Andrew, she tried to think of some way to convince their father to change his mind and let Charlotte marry first.

She doubted that begging would work. Besides,

Charlotte had tried that recently, to no avail. Perhaps if she sat down with some logical arguments, Father would listen. Maybe if she talked to Mother first . . .

Justine shook her head, and bent to smell a sprig of lilac. She closed her eyes and breathed deeply. The sweet, familiar scent flowed through her, soothing her jumbled emotions.

It also reminded her of her late night meeting with Andrew.

Justine forced herself back to thinking about Charlotte, and increased her pace through the garden. She expected that Mother would defer to Father on this matter. Mother would feel it was proper for Justine to marry first. It had been that way in her family, and Mother was proper in all things.

She considered the idea of telling Father of Charlotte's plan to elope.

No, that wouldn't work. Justine turned and paced back the way she had come. Besides betraying Charlotte's confidence, which she would be loathe to do, she was sure that would not change Father's mind. He would only be furious, and have Charlotte watched like a hawk. Perhaps he would send her back to their home in the country. Or forbid her to marry Kevin altogether, and choose another husband for her.

Justine sighed, and went to sit on a stone bench in the sunlight. The May morning was already warm as the sun moved toward its noon position, and the day promised a hotter afternoon.

She heard a laugh and recognized her brother George's tone. A moment later he rounded the corner on a run.

"Good morning," she greeted him fondly.

"Morning, Justine!" he called, dashing past her, his dark hair tousled.

He must be taking a break from lessons, Justine surmised.

Ah, to be as carefree as a youngster! She sighed, wishing she had no problems on which to dwell.

Impulsively, she sprang up and hurried after George. She found him hiding behind a tree.

"What are you doing?" she asked.

"Shh. I'm hiding from the French."

"The French?"

"I'm a spy," he hissed.

Ah, he was playing games. She smiled at her brother. "I will hide you, sir. When the French come, you can go down the cellar stairs."

Catching on to the fact that Justine was play-acting with him, George nodded. "They're coming this way."

They played for several minutes, until George told Justine he must be on his way, to bring a message to the king.

"Be careful," she told him in a serious voice before he dashed off.

She wandered back to the main path. The interlude with her brother had cleared her muddled thinking, and she returned to considering alternatives for Charlotte and Kevin.

Could she work on Charlotte and Kevin, and persuade them to postpone their marriage?

That seemed highly unlikely. Justine suspected that her romantic sister might be more determined than Kevin.

Perhaps if Kevin's father approached Roderick . . .

Justine doubted that would help. From her observations, Kevin's father, a minor country baron, had always been a little in awe of Roderick.

No, she must find some other way to approach the problem. If she couldn't convince Father—what other recourse did they have?

Perhaps none. Perhaps they would simply have to wait for her to marry—

Justine's thoughts seemed to stop dead.

Then they raced.

If she *did* have to marry first . . .

Or if she could *pretend* she was going to marry . . .

She walked more rapidly.

She could pretend she was going to get married. She was good at play-acting. She did it all the time with her younger siblings, as she had just now with George.

She could encourage, and accept, one of the suitors who was buzzing around her. And then, after a time, with Charlotte safely engaged, she could cry off.

It just might work.

She paused. Of course, she didn't want to hurt anyone. But she knew full well that most of the men who had expressed interest in her did so because she came from a noble family, and had money. Perhaps they also felt attracted to her. Perhaps they even had some liking for her. But none of them was in love.

She could put her plan in motion without worrying about breaking any hearts.

It just might work!

And right now, it was the only promising plan she could conjure up.

Justine moved down the path, with a determined step, and began to search for Charlotte.

She found her sister arranging some cut flowers in the small green parlor, which was in the section of the house that was sunny in the mornings but shaded and cool during the afternoons. Mother called it the summer room. Now, the late morning sun was streaming through the windows.

She glanced to the right and left. Charlotte was alone.

"I have a plan," she announced.

"You do?"

"Yes." Quickly, she told Charlotte her idea.

Charlotte's eyes grew wide. "But, Justine . . . I did not mean for you to get married just so I could!"

"Oh, I won't. I will cry off, but by then, your nuptials will be planned, and I doubt if Mother and Father would then expect you to postpone them."

Charlotte appeared more doubtful than Justine would have expected. "But, then how will you find a husband? People may talk, and say you are difficult to get along with. And other men will not gather around if they think you are engaged."

Justine shrugged. "People know I am not difficult; so I don't believe they will say that for long. Perhaps I will choose a man who is difficult himself." She turned, and paced up and down the room, warming to the idea. "That is it; I shall choose someone who is difficult to get along with. Perhaps Lord Mandershin or Sir Dothy . . . it would serve them right to be taken down a peg or two, they think overmuch of themselves."

"And what of finding your true love?" Charlotte persisted. She waved a yellow flower at Justine. "How will you do that if you are tied to another man?"

"Oh, it should be easy enough for me to move about socially," Justine said. But inside, she was not so sure. Charlotte had brought up a good point. She did want to get married eventually, and have a family. It could be harder to meet men this season if she was tied down to a fiancé.

She gave Charlotte a winning smile. "Please do not worry, Charlotte. I will begin to implement the plan tonight, at the ball at the Duke of Ashton's. I will choose a gentleman to spend a lot of time with. People will begin to talk, and when we become engaged, it will seem natural."

"Oh, Justine!" Charlotte dropped the flower on the table and threw her arms around Justine. "You are a wonderful sister. I will not forget this. Someday I will help you too."

Justine hugged her back, then smoothed Charlotte's dark blond hair off her face. "You promised me you wouldn't do anything rash, and I'm holding you to that."

"Of course I won't! I would not break a promise to you!" Her hazel eyes flashed.

"But you had promised not to meet Kevin alone in the garden—and you did."

"I promise I will not do anything rash," Charlotte repeated, looking so solemn Justine's tension began to dissipate.

"Now, can you get word to Kevin, so he knows what is going on? I don't know if he will be at the ball."

"He will be there with his parents, but I have a way

to get notes to him," Charlotte said, recovering the flower she'd dropped.

Justine did not ask how. She wasn't sure she wanted to know.

"Then it is settled," she said lightly.

But as she left the green room, she had an uncomfortable sensation in her stomach.

She was not so sure things were settled.

Who on earth was she to get temporarily engaged to?

Justine stood with several of her friends, scanning the crowded ballroom as she waved her fan back and forth. The Duke of Ashton's annual ball was in full swing, and the room was growing quite warm. Women in colorful gowns and men in brocaded vests moved from one group to another. Some danced and others bent their heads close, laughing together. The atmosphere was decidedly merry.

Beside Justine, her friends Selena and Jane were commenting and giggling over several dashing young men who had just entered the room.

Who was she to encourage? Who was she to choose? The questions played over and over in Justine's head so much that she barely paid heed to her friends' conversation.

Kevin had approached her almost at once and danced the first dance with her. He had been effusive, repeating Charlotte's comments of gratitude for her help with their marriage plans. They had gone for refreshments, and then Justine had suggested he leave her so she might find another gentleman to spend time with. Bowing and smiling, he had quickly complied.

Justine had danced next with Sir Marvin Dothy. He had been making comments of late about trying to get to know her better. While Justine had previously done nothing to encourage him, she'd decided to rectify that. Tonight she smiled widely and pretended to listen to his pontifications on several subjects after they danced. She knew his family did not have much money. He had made no secret among his peers that he intended to select a wife whose family would give her a sizable dowry. If the family was an old, noble one, like his own, so much the better.

Which meant Justine fit his needs exactly.

But could she stand being engaged, even for a short time, to such a boring man?

She had severe doubts.

Finally, she excused herself, and had exited to the ladies' retiring room for a few minutes.

She wished Charlotte was here to debate the merits of the men at the ball. She dared not speak to her friends about her plan. Dear friends that they were, neither Selena nor Jane were tight-lipped.

Returning to the ballroom, she had found Selena and Jane, and was glad enough for their company and amusing comments. As she stood with them now, half-listening, she scanned the throng for other possible suitors.

There was the Earl of Sommend's second son. He was a nice, mild young man . . . but Justine felt rather sorry for the shy young man, and would not want to ill-use him.

She fanned herself as the room grew warmer, casting about in her mind for another possible suitor.

"Oh, look over there," Jane said, pointing to the door. "It is the Marquis of Whitbury!" Her voice took on a dreamy note. "Wouldn't it be wonderful to garner his attention? He has money and a title, and he is handsome to boot."

"Yes, but every girl here has her eyes on him," Selena said with a sigh.

"Well, that does not mean he won't look at one of us. What do you think, Justine? Your family knows his," Jane asked, turning to her. "Was not your father a fast friend of his late father's?"

"Yes, indeed," murmured Justine, surprised at the little catch in her voice. And the accompanying ache inside her. She smiled briefly at her friends. "He is a nice person too."

"What are we waiting for?" Jane asked merrily. "Let's go speak to him."

"I believe I will get a breath of fresh air," Justine said. She needed some peace and time to herself. "You go ahead."

Andrew entered the crowded ballroom, already regretting his promise to the Duke of Ashton and his wife that he would attend their annual ball. Only the fact they had been close to his parents kept him from crying off. After his parents' deaths, the duke had assured him he could always count on him for friendship or advice; he had repeated those comments at Uncle Elias' and Cyril's funerals.

Andrew was thinking, however, of leaving early. On the way here, he had even considered a few excuses.

But in his carriage he had also mulled over the idea

of seeing Justine again, and continuing their sprightly conversation.

Now, as he looked over the noisy crowd, he found himself looking for a petite woman with a head of dark hair.

He spotted Roderick Rawlings and his wife, Mary. But Justine was not close by. He stepped forward, turning to look in the opposite direction. But as he did, he saw a determined-looking mama heading straight towards him.

He wheeled about and hurriedly exited the ballroom. Once in the corridor, he walked as quickly as he could past several chattering groups of men and women. He made his way further down the corridor. Perhaps he would find a room set up for card-playing. Although he had no great desire tonight for gaming, it might be preferable to avoiding the dozens of marriage-seeking, empty-headed women who had been pestering him of late. The corridor grew quieter as he reached the end. He was about to round a corner when a hushed voice from that area had him halting.

". . . you promised Mother . . . or don't you remember?" a man said.

"Yes, yes . . . I know I promised her I would wed a titled gentleman. And I was about to! When she died, she was rapturous that I was engaged to a marquis."

Even before hearing those last words, Andrew had recognized the voice. Isobel Newmont.

"But," Isobel continued, "it is not my fault that Cyril died before we were married."

"Now you must find another titled gentleman. A wealthy one. And fast!"

That had to be the voice of her brother, Darren.

Andrew had already known Isobel's designs on him were for selfish reasons. Loathe to listen to the rest of the conversation, he slowly stepped back.

"What about you?" she was snapping to her brother. "Why don't you become engaged and save us from the poorhouse? You're the one who has spent a great deal of money of late. There are heiresses aplenty here tonight."

"I have tried. Few heiresses have families that want them attached to a man with no title and little money. You, at least, have great beauty. It should be easy enough for you to find a wealthy fiancé—"

Andrew had taken another step back, but this time the wood beneath his feet creaked loudly.

"What's that?" Darren asked.

Andrew could hear Darren move. He did not want the disagreeable pair to know he had heard them, so he moved forward and called out "Edward! Is that you?" in a cheery voice, just as Darren turned the corner.

"My lord!" Isobel Newmont said in a plaintive voice.

She looked attractive enough in a gown of dark green, which was cut low. A feather in her fine blond hair added a little color to her pale face.

"Good evening," Andrew said, and bowed. "How are you this fine evening?" He wondered how soon he could make his escape.

"Not so well, my lord. I fear I am still quite beside myself over Cyril's untimely death." Her pointy chin rose, and she looked up at him. "I vow I could use some cheering up. I believe you said you could visit me one of these days soon?"

"I will try," Andrew replied slowly, doing his best to

be polite while not giving Isobel any hint of encouragement. He had discussed her forwardness with Edward only this morning. His friend had agreed with him that Isobel was, quite obviously, hoping to catch his interest and attain the title of marchioness that she had counted on when Cyril was alive.

"Better watch it, my friend," Edward had told him. "Isobel is trying to get her claws into you now that Cyril is gone."

"Not a chance," Andrew had retorted. He had never liked Isobel or her cold, calculating demeanor, despite the fact that she was a good-looking woman.

Now, as Isobel looked up at him expectantly, he decided to do what he had promised himself he would do yesterday—and be more forceful in his dealings with marriage-minded women. "As I explained yesterday, I am very busy with the demands of my estate. There is much to see to, with both my uncle's and Cyril's demises. It may take me weeks to catch up," he said, deliberately adopting a stern expression. An expression that verged on haughty, which he had seen on his uncle's face often enough. For good measure, he added, "You understand, of course, that for a gentleman who has recently inherited a title such as this, there is much to oversee."

Isobel instantly assumed a look of contrition. "Of course, my lord," she said, almost gushing. "You have much to do, it is true. It is only that I am so lonely—I thought perhaps we could visit and console each other in our time of grieving."

Her words were an echo of yesterday's. Andrew could imagine how she would try to console him. She was the kind of scheming woman who might try to end up in his arms, then have her brother walk in, declare that her reputation was compromised, and try to force Andrew to marry her. That is, if seduction didn't work. He guessed she would be willing to try one or the other.

"I must see someone now," he said, continuing with the cold tone Uncle Elias had often used. "Excuse me."

"Certainly, certainly," she said. "But I do hope to see you soon, my lord." She gave him a bright smile which Andrew found false and distasteful.

He gave a curt nod, then wound through the crowd. Acting like his uncle seemed to be a successful way to rid himself of Isobel, he thought. He would have to stick to that plan if she bothered him again. He dodged a determined-looking mother who was coming rapidly toward him, with another stern look on his face. He then looked around for Edward or Henry, or any of his other cronies. As he scanned the room, he found himself also looking for Justine.

"My lord! How wonderful to see you!" Miss Jane Perthing and Lady Selena Barton stopped him when he turned to look to his left.

"Good evening, ladies," he said pleasantly. As he gave a brief bow, he cast a look around. *Edward, where are you?*

"We were just talking about you," Lady Selena said, gushing almost as much as Isobel.

"Oh?" he asked politely. *Edward!* "What were you saying?"

Selena gaped at him. "Uh . . . that is . . ."

He saw Jane give Selena a discreet jab with her

elbow. "We were talking to our dear friend Justine," Jane said smoothly. "I believe her father was a friend of your late father."

Something akin to anticipation flowed through him. "Yes, the Rawlings are old friends. As a matter of fact, I was hoping to speak to Justine. Do you know where she is?"

The two young ladies exchanged a glance as stringed instruments began another dance. Selena began to fan herself. Then Jane said, "I believe she stepped out on the terrace," and pointed to a far corner of the ballroom.

"Thank you, ladies," Andrew said gallantly. He started forward when a hand was clapped on his shoulder.

"Andrew!" He was relieved to hear Edward's merry voice.

"Yes, my friend," Andrew said, equally jovial. Finally, some help in escaping the pursuing females!

He turned and found Edward's smile especially wide. His friend obviously knew he was getting tired of the many young ladies and mothers seeking his attention.

Edward guided him over to the side, where Henry and Carl Withsom, another acquaintance, were talking.

"Thank you," Andrew said in a low tone. "I am in need of rescuing tonight."

"Again," Edward added, and laughed. "Lord, Andrew, you can't walk two feet without being accosted by a young lady."

"Or her mama," Andrew said, shaking his head.

"It's not so terrible," Carl said. A quiet young man, he was rather shy and often unnoticed at gatherings.

"I will be glad to introduce you to some of these young ladies," Andrew offered.

"Why not tell them he has a veritable fortune?" Henry suggested. "That will accomplish two things: Carl will get some attention—and it will take the light off you."

"Good idea," Andrew said.

"No, you can't—" Carl began.

"Have no fear, I will introduce you to someone nice," Andrew said. "Not someone like Isobel."

Edward shuddered. "That one is cold as ice," he said, his tone low.

"And I don't trust her," Andrew added.

"You shouldn't." Edward's voice dropped to a whisper, and he repeated his warning of this morning. "Watch out. I think she is one of the most scheming females in existence."

"I well believe it." Andrew meant never to spend any time alone with Isobel. Or any time with her in a crowd either.

As he conversed with his friends, he cast glances about periodically for Justine. He was disappointed to see no sign of her. He wondered if he could dance with her without causing much speculation.

"Look out," Henry said suddenly. "Here come several mothers and daughters. And they're aiming straight for you, Andrew."

The particular group headed toward them was especially determined—two matrons who were cousins, one with an eligible daughter and the other with two marriage-minded daughters. Even the group of men surrounding him did not seem to dissuade them from their quest.

Thanking his friends, Andrew made a quick getaway

toward the French doors. He wondered if the women would try to corner Edward, Henry and Carl. They were wealthy bachelors too, although untitled.

On the terrace, a woman with dark hair, in a gown of buttercup yellow, was gazing out over the gardens.

Justine.

His step quickened.

Justine stood in a shadowy corner of the large terrace, looking out over one of the most beautiful landscapes in England. The Duke of Ashton was proud of the gardens which had been in his family for centuries. It was said that the duke spared no expense in its upkeeping. And the duchess was greatly interested in roses and encouraged the gardeners to try the newer, different varieties. In addition, the maze here was one of the finest and most complex that Justine had ever seen.

Justine took a deep breath. Even though the first rose bushes were several yards away, there were so many beginning to bloom that the scent filled the night. She found it delightful.

But the gardens were not foremost in her thoughts. Beneath the moonlight, with the warm air humming with the sounds of the ball, Justine struggled with her problem.

Who to select as a temporary fiancé? *Who?*

She was beginning to regret her impulsive idea to help Charlotte. Perhaps she had gone too far in coming to her sister's aid.

Still, the alternative—Charlotte running away to Gretna Green for a hasty marriage—was unthinkable.

Justine again ran through a list of possible suitors in her mind, as she'd done before, rejecting them one by one. Either they were men she didn't want to hurt, didn't think she could stand for even a brief engagement, or were unlikely to propose.

Without volition, her mind wandered to Andrew Pennington.

Andrew? No, he had made it quite clear he was uninterested in marriage, at least for the present.

Besides, the vexing young man he had been had probably not changed overmuch. He would still be a constant tease, tormenting her no end, she suspected.

Justine sighed deeply, and allowed herself a brief moment of pity. Why could she not let things run their course, and when the time seemed right, choose a husband who was suitable, someone she liked and admired, and could see herself living with for the rest of her life?

Perhaps, she thought, she would have to tell Charlotte she was changing her mind?

She heard a footfall behind her, and straightened her back, prepared to fend off some unwanted attention.

"I was hoping to find you here," a deep, laughter-filled voice said.

Justine whirled to face Andrew, her heart beating quickly at the sound of his voice. It seemed even deeper than it had at the musicale.

"Oh!" The gladness that washed over her was a surprise. For a moment she could think of nothing to say. All she could do was to smile at Andrew, who had appeared, as if out of the mist of her daydreams. "Good evening," she murmured, getting hold of herself. Her voice trembled slightly and she bit her lip. She was not going to act like one of the moonstruck young ladies who had been fawning at his feet since he arrived at the ball.

"I had hoped to continue yesterday's conversation," Andrew said in a good-humored voice. "I—is there something wrong?" His voice dropped. He stepped closer, and putting a finger to her chin, tilted it up. A little spark shimmered up her spine. Justine's lips parted.

She had never had a man touch her face before. That must be why she felt this jolt of energy.

"You are crying," Andrew said, his voice husky with concern. "Why?"

Too late, Justine realized a tear had slid down her cheek. She went to brush it away with her fingers. Andrew was staring at her intently, frowning, his blue eyes reflecting concern.

"I'm–I'm fine," she said, her voice shaky.

"Tell me what is wrong."

"It's . . . it has to do with my sister Charlotte," Justine said. She shouldn't spill the story out to him, but he looked so sympathetic, and she could use a friend. "But I can't talk about it."

"You can talk to me," Andrew said, leaning closer. "Come, let's walk in the gardens, so no one else will overhear." Once again he took her hand and placed it through his arm. And once again she went along with him, feeling strangely comforted and relieved by his presence.

They walked down stone steps and along the pathway. Where it forked, the sweet scent of roses enveloped them. Andrew took the path to the right, and they entered the maze.

Once cloaked among the tall bushes, Andrew spoke again. "Please tell me what is wrong. I am your friend and a friend of your family's; perhaps I can help."

Doubts assailed Justine. "There is nothing . . . wrong."

"Come now, Justine. If it is enough to make you cry, then surely you could use some help in figuring out how to solve the problem."

She surely could! Stopping to gaze at Andrew, she realized it might help to get some advice. Sometimes another view, that of someone more objective, could help in addressing a problem. Perhaps he could come up with a better plan to handle this situation than she had.

"I will tell you but—you must promise not to repeat this. If my father should find out . . . he will be very angry with Charlotte."

"Of course I will not repeat it. Come, there is a bench around the next turn."

Andrew led her through part of the maze into a small opening. A stone bench was placed there, and they seated themselves. In the moonlight, Andrew's face looked particularly handsome, and utterly sympathetic. Justine felt instinctively that she could trust him.

"Charlotte wants to marry Kevin . . ." Justine began, and spilled out the entire story. She finished with her own idea for getting their father's approval for Charlotte and Kevin to set a wedding date soon. Justine found herself twisting her fingers, and had to force herself to let them rest in her lap.

Andrew listened, asking only one or two questions.

"And I do not want to hurt a fine man's sensibilities,"

she finished, "by breaking an engagement if he has . . . grown fond of me."

When she finished, Andrew appeared to be thinking. The next words out of his mouth were quite shocking.

"Why not me?"

Chapter Five

*A*ndrew?

Had Justine heard him correctly?

"I beg your pardon?"

"Why not pretend an engagement to me?" Andrew asked.

"To you?" She sat back, stunned, staring at his face. Could this be another of his infamous teasing jokes?

He appeared to be sincere. But experience had taught Justine that Andrew could look serious, and then burst into laughter seconds later.

"You're joking, my lord," she said crisply.

But he shook his head. "No. This idea makes sense. If I become party to your scheme, you will not have to worry about hurting somebody's sensibilities, because I will be aware of the reasons."

Her heart accelerated. "But you . . . you do not want to marry yet! You said so yourself, yesterday. That presently, you wanted to be left alone." Could he possibly be serious?

"And this would be the perfect way to discourage all those young ladies who are pursuing me," Andrew declared, enthusiasm igniting his voice. "Yes, this would be a perfect plan! If I am engaged, they would not keep running after me. I would finally be left alone."

Justine stared at Andrew, the light in his eyes, the smile tilting his mouth. He appeared to be genuinely excited about her plan.

Could this be the solution she had hoped for? But it seemed almost too neat. She opened her mouth, then closed it.

Perhaps it would work!

A plan such as this would suit them both well. They could pretend to get engaged, Charlotte could go on to marry Kevin, Andrew would be free of the hovering ladies, and Justine could relax and enjoy her season. And decide later who she really wanted to marry.

Well, why not?

"It appears," Justine said slowly, "that you have had a brilliant idea, my lord. It will solve Charlotte's problem, help you to be free of your ... shall we say, unwelcome pursuers? I can enjoy the season and decide at my leisure who shall be my future spouse."

"Call me Andrew. We are friends, remember, and soon-to-be engaged. Will you accept my suit?" He smiled at her, a curiously eager and boyish expression lighting his face.

"Yes," she answered simply. Oddly, a strange sensation swept through her. Anticipation?

He flashed her a smile. "Perfect. This should help us both immensely."

"Wait," she said, as a thought occurred to her. "Andrew, our families are friends—how can we put off a wedding until after Charlotte marries Kevin? My parents will want to start making plans at once."

"But I am in mourning for my uncle and cousin," Andrew said, his eyes gleaming in the moonlight. An insect buzzed by, but the sound was subdued. "They will not expect me to make plans straight away."

"That is true," she said thoughtfully. "Of course, it is I who will have to end the engagement . . . otherwise our reputations will both be tarnished if you do so."

"Yes. But if you cry off, then people will assume I am difficult, and not be so eager to pursue me!" He chuckled. "That will be good indeed for me. So, may I call upon your father tomorrow and ask for your hand?"

"Yes."

Andrew took hold of her hand. Bending forward, he kissed the tips of her fingers, pressing them firmly with his warm lips.

A thrill unlike anything Justine had ever felt before swept through her, leaving her tingling from her fingers down to her toes.

As Andrew straightened, his eyes met hers, and held.

They stared at each other in the soft moonlight, the warm May evening caressing them like a lover's tender touch.

Justine felt as if the breath had been taken from her.

He stood and she sat rooted in place for a moment.

And then Andrew gave her his teasing grin. "Isn't this romantic?"

"Romantic? Your smile is positively mischievous," Justine remarked, quelling a feeling of disappointment at his usual teasing demeanor.

"Shall we return to the party?" he asked, more quietly. "And I venture to say it would be safe enough to spend some time together. I believe your father will accept my suit, and we can announce our plans after my meeting with him tomorrow."

As Justine let Andrew lead her back through the maze, her heart was beating quite hard, and she felt almost light-headed.

It's the moonlight, she told herself. And the rose-scented air. And the fact that she had just had a most dashing gentleman kiss her hand. All of those factors were causing this upheaval to her senses.

She should feel relieved, now that the problem of Charlotte would be solved.

But instead, she felt unsteady, as if she was teetering on the edge of a cliff, about to tumble.

Asking for a woman's hand in marriage was not an easy task, Andrew decided as he entered Roderick's study.

Especially since he was filled with a mixed bag of emotions.

He had been both excited by Justine's plan and relieved, since by declaring himself to be her fiancé, it would keep the pursuing mamas and daughters away. And he was happy to help Justine as a friend.

But something had happened during their moments together in the garden. When he'd kissed her hand, he'd felt something . . . indefinable. He struggled for a moment to name the peculiar feeling.

It was more than mere attraction. For several seconds, the very air about them had seemed to glow.

Indeed, for a moment it had all seemed unbelievably real. Like he was truly becoming engaged to the lovely, warm and spirited woman who sat with him in the garden, an almost bemused expression on her face.

Then he'd realized that it was merely play-acting, and before the scene became too melodramatic, he'd deliberately broken the tension with a quip and laughter.

Yet now, he felt an unaccustomed uneasiness as he seated himself across from Roderick. In the somber study, Roderick looked an imposing figure behind his huge desk.

"Now, is there some way I can help you?" Roderick asked, leaning forward. "Advice I can give you, perhaps, regarding your late uncle's estates?" His tone was kind, and so was his expression.

Andrew switched his position in the comfortable leather chair, feeling curiously young. "I thank you for the offer. I much appreciate your help with the funeral arrangements for my uncle and cousin. You are the first one I will come to for further advice the moment I need it."

"I will be glad to give it. Your father, William, would have done the same for my sons Walter and George if I was the one who had passed on first." He leaned back in his chair. "Please call on me any time. Your father was as close to me as any of my brothers. Perhaps more so. And I am sure your uncle would want you to turn to family friends for guidance, since this is a job for which you were not totally prepared. Of course you have managed your late father's estates well—but your uncle's holdings are vast, and it was a surprise to you to inherit."

"I appreciate that." There was a brief silence. "I am here on another matter," he continued cautiously.

"Yes?"

"It has to do with . . . Justine." He cleared his throat.

"What about Justine?" Roderick asked, raising his eyebrows.

"I would—" Lord, this was tougher than he would have thought! He sat forward. "I would like to ask for her hand in marriage." He swallowed.

A sudden look of delight overtook Roderick's face, leaving no doubt as to his feelings.

Andrew felt compelled to list his attributes. "I believe I would be a suitable husband. I come from a noble family, as you know, and I have more than enough money to see that Justine's life would be most comfortable. I will be a loyal husband, and take good care of her."

"I will be proud to have you as a son-in-law!" Roderick said, beaming. "And I know Mary will feel likewise. It is what your father and I always hoped for."

"It is?" Andrew asked, startled. He sat back in the chair.

"Yes, indeed. Many times William and I would sit here, in this very room, in those chairs by the window." He waved to two deep leather chairs. "And we would talk about the hope that one day our families would be connected. In fact, the day you put an insect or worm or some such thing on Justine's bonnet, William predicted that she would be the one of my daughters who would catch your fancy."

"My father said that?" Andrew was astonished. He knew his father had been fond of Roderick's children; but he had never suspected that William wished him to marry one of Roderick's daughters. Or that he had predicted that it would be Justine who caught his attention.

"Yes, indeed. This calls for a toast." Roderick walked to the sideboard and lifted a cut crystal decanter. It glinted in the sunlight. Pouring two small glasses that sat on a tray, he handed one to Andrew, who rose. "I shall call Mary down presently, but first . . ." He lifted his glass of sherry. "To the happy joining of our two noble families!"

"To our families," Andrew seconded, and lifted his glass. Their glasses touched with a ping, and he sipped the sherry.

"Of course," Andrew said, returning to his seat, the glass still in his hand, "I must pay my addresses to Justine. I hope she will look favorably on my suit."

"I believe she will," Roderick said, taking his seat too. "I watched her yesterday when you were dancing with her at the ball. Mary said at the time that she thought Justine was paying more attention to you than to any of the other young men who've been pursuing her. We had never seen her regard any potential suitors thusly. I admit we wondered if something would come of it." Roderick placed his glass on his desk. "Justine is a sweet, intelligent, warm-hearted young woman. She will make a good wife. Of course, you must be the one to ask her directly; but I believe she'll accept your suit."

His smile deepened. "Now, I am sure you are eager to see her. I will ring for a servant to check on her whereabouts; but I think she was in the morningroom with her sister Charlotte and my wife just a short while ago." He got up and pulled the thick bellpull. "Shall I ask her to meet you in the library? It is a favorite room of hers."

"Certainly, sir," Andrew said, standing up. He added one more thing. "Since I am in mourning, the wedding will have to be after a suitable period."

"Of course."

They shook hands, Roderick still smiling broadly. Andrew left the room moments later, smiling himself. He proceeded down the hall to the stately library.

He placed his hand on the knob, and paused.

In his nervous excitement—or whatever one would call it—he realized he had forgotten something.

He had forgotten that his engagement to Justine was not real.

Justine had been trying to listen with half an ear to the sounds outside the morningroom as she worked on her embroidery. Usually she enjoyed the work, finding it could be most soothing. But today she felt on edge, and supposed it was because she was waiting to find out what was transpiring between her father and Andrew.

She had heard Andrew's arrival twenty minutes ago. So when the butler entered the morningroom with the request from her father that Justine report to the library, she was not surprised.

Justine's mother looked surprised, however, when Danvers told her, "Madam, Mr. Rawlings wishes you to join him in his study."

Mary put aside her own embroidery. "Certainly." Casting a quizzical glance at Justine, she walked out of the room, moving with a firm but unhurried step.

Charlotte, who had been rearranging some flowers, shot a hopeful glance at Justine. Justine smiled briefly and left the room, trying to match her mother's unhurried stride.

It was hard to keep a composed demeanor. She wanted to move quickly, and her heart was beating rapidly.

She entered the library and found Andrew gazing at a shelf of volumes.

"You wished to see me, my lord?" she asked formally, striving to keep her voice calm.

Andrew turned, grinning. He strode toward Justine and reached for her hands.

"Our plan is working," he said in a low voice. "Your father has approved my suit."

"Oh, ahh . . . very good." Justine's heart did not slow down, however. If anything, with her hands clasped within Andrew's warm, strong ones, her heart had accelerated.

"I am now formally paying my addresses to you," he added, a mischievous glint in his eyes.

"You look rather jovial for a man proposing," Justine said. She smiled, trying to mirror his expression, but her smile felt forced.

He raised his eyebrows. "This is what you wanted, is it not?"

She nodded. It *was* what she had wished for.

"And I am accepting." The words came out breathlessly.

Andrew squeezed her hands, and for a long moment, they stared at each other.

"The only problem is . . ." Andrew frowned suddenly. "When you do cry off from our engagement—and we've agreed you should be the one to do so—your father may be quite disappointed. He said he had always hoped for a match between our families."

"Oh?" Justine should have guessed that, she thought with chagrin. "Well, I will invent some plausible excuse, a disagreement or something. After Charlotte and Kevin set their date. We can discuss it later."

Andrew still had hold of her hands, and Justine found the tingling in them most unusual.

"Fine. Now, to make this look authentic"—and once again she saw the distinct, mischievous glint in his eye—"perhaps we should embrace?"

"I . . ." Justine's voice faded. She could not think of one thing to say. She felt frozen to the spot. Her heart beat faster.

She *wanted* him to embrace her.

He pulled her closer, and kissed her on the forehead gently. His lips were warm. Justine closed her eyes, wishing for one moment to simply enjoy the feel of a man's kiss. The unique experience. She felt herself beginning to relax.

Andrew tightened his hands on hers. His lips moved down her cheek, still gently, then reached her mouth.

She made a slight sound of surprise, and then his lips touched hers, tenderly.

Suddenly Justine was no longer relaxed. Her whole body tensed.

She had always wondered what her first kiss would be like. She had thought it would be sweet.

But it was more.

She had not expected his lips to be smooth but firm. And they were warm. Oh, they were quite warm!

His hands drew her closer, and they dropped hers and surrounded her waist. His lips pressed against hers, harder.

And everything surrounding her faded. She was aware only of Andrew, of his hands on her waist, of his lips pressed against hers, his skin brushing hers as he angled his head.

Her heart jumped and galloped away.

For several moments she stood locked in his embrace, reveling in the unexpected sensations. And then she found herself kissing him back.

When Andrew raised his head she felt almost dizzy, and wavered. He loosened his hold gradually, gazing at her.

Before she could say anything more, Andrew grinned, reached down and ruffled her hair.

"Andrew!" It came out as a squeak.

"We must make this look authentic," he said, laughing. "If you look too neat, no one will believe we were . . . um . . . in each other's arms."

"I'm sure my father would not expect us to act so . . ." Justine grasped for the right words. "In–in such an unseemly manner!" She stepped back, trying to smooth her hair. Her heart beat wildly, and she noted her hands were trembling. She hid them behind her full skirt.

"I do not think he will mind your giving your fiancé a small kiss."

"That was not small!" Justine protested, trying to collect her scattered thoughts. She felt her cheeks grow hot. No, it was not small. The kiss was more like a clap of thunder.

"No, it wasn't." Andrew's expression suddenly grew serious. "I beg your pardon. I got . . . carried away, I suppose."

"You . . . did indeed," Justine chastised him. But inside she felt almost disappointed. It was preposterous but . . . for a moment she wanted him to kiss her again!

"I will take my leave then," Andrew said, stepping back. "I expect we will make the formal announcement very quickly." For a moment he gazed at her, and Justine wondered if he had the tiniest urge to embrace her once more. Then he gave her a formal bow. "Good day, Justine."

"Good day." Her voice was a whisper as she curtsied.

Andrew departed. Justine sank into her favorite dark red chair.

She had been kissed. By Andrew, of all people.

And she had *liked* it. She *liked* being held in his arms.

What was she getting herself into? Andrew was her temporary fiancé.

But she found herself wondering when he would kiss her again.

During the next week, Justine felt as if a whirlwind had entered her life and was carrying her about hither and yon. She was unprepared for the grand fuss that was being made about her engagement, and was quite amazed by it.

Her mother was bustling about with a new purpose, calling in merchants and consulting on everything from new gowns and hats to desserts.

"But Andrew is in mourning," Justine pointed out. "We cannot marry yet."

"Yes, but we must begin making plans!" her mother had said briskly. "And now we have Charlotte to consider as well."

Charlotte had lost no time in pressing their parents to allow her to come out right away; and to follow her debut with her own engagement announcement. Roderick had consented to Charlotte's betrothal so quickly that Justine knew he must be thrilled at the idea of her own marriage to Andrew, and so was in a most agreeable state of mind regarding all other matters.

It also seemed that everyone in town needed to stop by and wish the future Marchioness of Whitbury well. Dozens of the ton's finest nobles, including people Justine had barely spoken to, called upon her family at home to express their congratulations. Her parents knew most and greeted them calmly and cordially, but there had been such a steady stream that Justine could hardly remember them all. After three days, she asked her mother if she could take a respite.

"You are to be a marchioness," Mary pointed out. "You must get used to entertaining, Justine."

"But . . . all at once?"

Her mother's expression softened. "I know you are not used to this intensity of company. And every lady must have some time to call her own. Very well, tomorrow we will say you are not home and you may have some time to rest. We can't have you growing fatigued."

"Thank you, Mother."

Mary gave her a big smile. "I am so glad, Justine, that you found a husband who is not only *most* suitable, but for whom you have a deep affection. I knew at once you liked Andrew, and hoped he would want you for his wife." She gave her daughter a reminiscent smile. "It was just so with Roderick and I."

"Did you . . . love each other?" Justine asked tentatively.

"We had a deep respect and affection for each other. Love came later, after we married. I am sure the same will happen to you."

"What about . . . Charlotte and Kevin? They seem to love each other already."

"Yes, love matches do happen occasionally. Fortunately, Charlotte fell in love with someone who, while not quite the 'catch' Andrew is, still comes from a good family and is a suitable gentleman." She smiled. "I am most happy, dear. For both of you. And with luck, Ginette and Arabella will make good matches when the time arrives. In fact, since you have made such a brilliant match, it should be easier for your sisters to find suitable men."

"And Walter and George?" Justine pressed on. This was turning into a fascinating discussion.

"Oh, your brothers will have no trouble finding wives," her mother said, waving a hand. "It is easier for men, especially when they have money, as we do." Seeing something in Justine's face, she added, "I am convinced that Andrew would have offered for you even if we had little money. We are a noble family, and close to his own. And he seems to be . . . enamored of you. I have watched his expression when he is near you these last few days. Yes, indeed, he has an affection for you which I am sure will lead to love. And I can see in your eyes how much affection you have for him."

Startled, Justine could only stare at her mother.

Affection? For Andrew?

She thought about her mother's words as her mother looked at sketches brought over by the seamstress' assistant.

She had tried to hold off on selecting new gowns, reminding her mother that Andrew was in mourning; but her mother claimed that they had to start. Justine had told herself that she would use the new wardrobe when she did, someday, really marry.

As usual, her thoughts returned to Andrew. He had been on her mind constantly during this last week. And so had the kiss he'd given her. She could not restrain herself from replaying those moments in her mind. Over and over.

And part of her wished it would happen again.

He had limited his kisses to quick ones on her hand during the last few days. But several times his eyes had sparkled as they met hers, and she'd felt an answering glow deep inside. It could be affection, she realized.

Could Andrew harbor an affection for her as well?

One week after her engagement announcement, Justine sat with her sister and several friends in a corner of the lovely garden at Chetsworth Manor. The weather was warm but not overly so, and they were talking and giggling in the sunshine while their mothers and several older women occupied the terrace closer to the manor. Everyone's spirits were high and Justine was enjoying the afternoon.

It had been decided that Charlotte could accompany Justine and their mother to the afternoon garden party. Charlotte would be coming out in another week, but the party was at their Aunt Belinda's home just outside of London. Belinda, one of Mary's sisters, was married to the Earl of Chetsworth, and Mary had declared that since the garden party was at a relative's home, it would be considered acceptable for Charlotte to accompany them.

Charlotte was thrilled to finally attend a social function among the ton. Justine had been just as glad to go, because for the last two days their mother had been busy dragging them to dressmakers on Bond Street. Charlotte must have clothes for her coming out and future marriage; and of course Justine must have more clothes befitting her station as the future wife of a marquis.

Justine felt uncomfortable as the center of attention, especially since she knew it wouldn't last. But she had to admit that Charlotte was enjoying herself.

"Tell us," Selena was saying now, leaning closer to Justine, "just how did the marquis propose to you, Justine?" She tapped her fan against Justine's knee.

Justine smoothed her hand along her sky blue gown, searching for a vague way to answer her friend's question.

"Perhaps Justine wants that to remain private," Charlotte said, casting a glance at her older sister.

"Yes, just how were you able to snare him?" Lady Myrna, a rather snide young woman, asked Justine.

"I did not have to snare him, as you say," Justine said, her voice taking on a heated note. She had never cared for Lady Myrna, the rather stuckup daughter of a viscount. "He pursued me." Seeing the young woman's doubtful expression, she added, "We have known each other for years, after all; it is no surprise that we should make a match."

"You must tell us how he proposed!" Sophie, another acquaintance, begged eagerly.

"Yes, please do," several young ladies chorused.

Justine began slowly, making a mental note to herself to go over her story with Andrew in case he was asked the same. "It was in a most practical manner," she said. She took a deep breath, inhaling the scent of the fresh lilacs near her bench.

"Practical!" Her friend Jane looked disappointed.

"Yes, the marquis is a practical man," Justine said. "He simply suggested it would be sensible for us to marry. Since our families are both old, noble ones."

"And have been friends for ages," Charlotte added, scooting closer to Justine.

"But we had heard he was not in a rush to pick a bride," Sophie said. "My brother said that the marquis had said so, at his club, shortly after his uncle and cousin passed on. He must have fallen in love with you!" she added gleefully.

"How romantic!" exclaimed Jane.

There was a pause, and several birds chirped.

"Still, he did say he was in no hurry to marry," Lady Myrna continued, a dubious look on her face.

Justine's cousin Adelaide, who had been silent until now, spoke up. "He probably decided that as a marquis, it was time that he took a bride. And he knew Justine will make an excellent marchioness!" She smiled at her cousin.

Justine smiled back. Adelaide, a rather outspoken young woman, had always been a favorite cousin of hers. And now more so than ever.

"I can not think of anyone who would be more suitable," Adelaide continued, giving Lady Myrna a rather superior glance. "It is a most estimable match."

"That is so," Jane said, also giving Lady Myrna a disparaging look. "Justine comes from one of the most noble families of the ton; she is pretty and sweet—and has many suitors. If you ask me, Andrew will count himself lucky."

Justine was grateful for her friends' loyalty. She also had to repress a laugh. There was no use making it worse for Lady Myrna, who had few friends anyway.

Lady Myrna flushed at Jane's words. "I still think it is rather surprising."

Justine changed the subject. "I hear, Selena, that my cousin Marcus called on you just the other day." Marcus, Adelaide's oldest brother, had been attending parties recently. Adelaide had whispered to Justine and Charlotte that she thought he was beginning to look for a bride.

Selena flushed prettily. "Yes, and he is such merry company! We talked of many things." She glanced at Adelaide.

"He is one of our favorite cousins," Justine added with a smile. She stole a glance at Lady Myrna, who appeared to be sulking. Myrna's mouth was a thin line.

"Pray tell, what is this I hear about a possible match for you?" Sophie asked suddenly, turning to Charlotte.

"I . . . um . . ."

"Charlotte has already been pursued by a number of gentlemen," Justine quickly declared, watching her sister's face color. "My sister is one of the prettiest, kindest young ladies in London; it would not be surprising if she makes a match in the near future."

Justine had a feeling Charlotte had been talking to her friends. Although she had almost certainly asked them to keep the knowledge of her upcoming nuptials to themselves until after her debut and the planned announcement in a few weeks, it seemed as though someone had let the news slip out. Justine was not surprised. Any match, especially a love match, was fodder for the gossip mills in London.

"And what of you, Sophie?" Adelaide adeptly turned the conversation away from Charlotte. "I hear tell that a certain gentleman danced with you three times the other evening!"

Sophie smiled. "Yes, and Sir Marvin Dothy called on me only yesterday."

"Hmph. That's not much of a compliment," Lady Myrna said in her most catty voice. "Sir Marvin is looking for an heiress."

Sophie turned red. But her friends instantly came to her defense.

"That was uncalled for," Adelaide said sharply, snapping her fan. "Sir Marvin is a nice man."

Justine was growing tired of Myrna's nasty comments. "Who has called upon you lately?" she demanded of the sarcastic young woman.

"I'll have you know—" Myrna began.

Something whizzed by Justine, in between her and Charlotte, narrowly missing her arm. She felt the stir of air and heard a whistling sound.

Several of the young women gasped.

"What was that?" cried Charlotte.

"Oh my!" Selena exclaimed, jumping up.

Justine turned. Stuck in the tree right behind her was a long arrow.

A very long arrow.

It had nearly hit her or Charlotte.

Adelaide leaped up as well. "I'll get someone." She raced off, calling "Mother! Mother!"

"Where did it come from?" Justine asked, springing up. She moved to look at the arrow.

"Who could be hunting here?" Jane was demanding.

At the same time, Charlotte exclaimed, "It nearly hit us, Justine!"

"Oh . . ." Sophie said.

"Watch out! She's swooning!" Selena cried.

Commotion erupted as Sophie fainted. Justine and Jane both reached her in time to prevent her from toppling out of her chair. As they did, Jane began calling for help.

Casting a look around, Justine saw that Charlotte and several others had turned pale. She helped Jane lean Sophie's limp form back into the chair. Selena waved her fan over the young woman.

Groomsmen began to run towards them, followed by Justine's mother, aunt and some of the older women. One of the women also fainted when she saw the arrow.

In between the questions and exclamations, Justine

looked to see from where the marksman might have shot the arrow. There was a clump of trees nearby, and the direction the arrow had taken seemed to indicate it had come from there. But why would someone be shooting so close to the gardens? Carelessness? Or something else?

Justine could not suppress sudden shivers.

She shaded her eyes, turning to look about. But she could see nothing unusual.

"Justine, Charlotte, are you unharmed?" their mother was asking. Lady Selena had been recounting how the arrow had passed right between the sisters.

"Yes, quite fine," Justine said. She glanced at Charlotte, who still looked frightened.

"Do you think this was an accident?" Charlotte asked.

"Perhaps . . . or perhaps it was something more." Justine looked again at where the arrow protruded from the tree.

"I shall send for the earl immediately," Lady Chetsworth declared, placing her arms around her nieces.

Justine's imagination was taking flight. What if the arrow was aimed at Charlotte, or her? But who on earth would want to injure one of them?

She took a moment to imagine the arrow being aimed at Lady Myrna.

That young lady was now twittering away.

"We all might have been hurt!" she cried dramatically. "Someone has been very careless!"

Justine spotted the annoyed look her aunt sent

Myrna, before she quickly smoothed over her expression and turned to the others.

Myrna's mother sent her daughter a quelling look as well. "I'm sure the earl will discover who is behind this, Myrna." She had enough sense, Justine thought, to prefer not to offend the wife of an earl.

"Mama, we might have been gravely wounded!" Myrna complained.

"That is enough," Myrna's mother hissed, then took a firm hold of her daughter's arm. "I am so sorry, Lady Chetsworth, it appears my daughter is rather overcome and may be on the verge of passing out. Perhaps I should take her inside."

"That would be a good idea," Justine's aunt agreed. "We do not want hysterics. I am sure my husband will get to the bottom of this in no time."

Myrna's mother led her away.

Justine turned to look at the arrow again, as everyone continued to talk.

Had this been a random accident?

Or had it been aimed at Charlotte?

Or herself?

Andrew stared at the arrow on a table in the small study off the Earl of Chetsworth's massive library. Justine's uncle, the earl, was pointing to it as he spoke, his voice angry.

"It seems," the earl said, "that my groom was right. There is a substance at the end of the arrow, although I don't know what it is."

"This is most disturbing," Roderick Rawlings said.

He turned to look at the others gathered in the room. "It appears that this arrow may be poisoned."

Andrew frowned. There was silence among the men, and then Roderick spoke again. "Who could have shot an arrow—a poisoned arrow—near a party of young ladies? Who could be so careless?"

"If it was carelessness," the earl said. "My fear is that it was a deliberate attempt to injure one of the young ladies."

There were disturbed mutters among the men.

"If you are right," Andrew said, "then it seems that either Justine, or Charlotte, was the target of this marksman, since the arrow landed between them. He intended to injure one of them."

The earl looked from Andrew to Roderick. "I share your concern," he said staunchly. "They are not just your daughters, Roderick, but your intended and her sister," he said, nodding to Andrew, "*and* my nieces as well! I can assure you, we shall not rest until we find the culprit. Even now, I have my most trusted servants interviewing the household to see if anyone has information of any kind."

"I thank you," Andrew said.

"Yes, and I plan to send my men round to help," Roderick declared. "They can make inquiries in the neighborhood."

"And Edward and I will help as well," Andrew said, as Edward nodded in agreement. As soon as he had received word about the arrow, he had asked for Edward's help and the two had ridden over to see what they could do.

"I am most concerned," Andrew continued. "If it was

a careless error by a hunter who realizes he had made a grave mistake and is now trying to hide his identity, that is one thing. But if this was a deliberate attempt to injure one of the party, that is most serious. Especially since this marksman will discover he did not succeed. That means he may make a similar attempt in the future."

The men gathered around the table nodded, their expressions grim.

"We will have to watch over our daughters carefully," Roderick said.

"In fact, we must all be on our guard," the earl stated.

There were sounds of agreement.

"Is there a way to identify the arrow?" Edward asked.

The earl shook his head. "No one here has been able to. But I am sending for a physician. My hope is he may be able to recognize what is on the arrow."

The men spoke for several minutes, suggesting several possibilities. Then the earl and Roderick went off to supervise the questionings, and the rest of the men departed.

As they got ready to mount their horses, Edward said in a low voice to Andrew, "You appear to be most anxious about this incident, and about Justine's welfare."

"Of course." Seeing the quizzical look on Edward's face, he added, "She is my friend, Edward." He had told Edward, in strictest confidence, what was behind his engagement. Growing up, the two had shared secrets, and he knew Edward could be trusted.

Edward raised his eyebrows now but said nothing.

A stableboy approached and, as he held the horse, Andrew mounted. He waited for Edward, and then the two trotted off to return to their club, where Andrew intended to start inquiries. He had thought to start with people who were excellent marksmen and hunters to ask if anyone knew what substance might be put at the end of an arrow.

He thought about Edward's remark as they rode. Yes, of course he was concerned about Justine—and Charlotte as well. They might have been the targets of an evil person.

Andrew did not know why the girls might be targets, unless Roderick had some unknown enemy who was trying to get revenge. He mulled over that thought, finally putting it aside as unlikely. Roderick Rawlings led an exemplary life; it was doubtful that anyone would resent him enough to do something of this sort.

His fears for Justine grew as they trotted down the peaceful lane that would turn into a major street in London within several miles.

Justine was sweet and innocent and might easily become a target again. He would have to watch out for her welfare, protect her, and when they married, he would have to make sure she was well chaperoned.

When they married?

He could almost hear Edward voicing the thought. But it came from his own mind.

He was not going to be marrying Justine. Theirs was a temporary engagement.

And yet, the thought of being married to Justine lingered.

And oddly enough, Andrew found the thought to be surprisingly pleasant.

Hesston Public Library
P.O. Box 640
110 East Smith
Hesston, KS 67062

Chapter Six

Justine was surprised when Andrew visited her the next evening.

After the commotion of the last few weeks and the disturbing event during the garden party, she had been happy to spend a quiet evening at home. She'd been sitting in the library, enjoying a romantic novel full of spirited characters and intrigue, when Danvers announced in his most formal tones that Lord Andrew Pennington, the Marquis of Whitbury, was here to call upon her.

Justine hurriedly smoothed her hair and went to the blue parlor, where Andrew was waiting.

"Good evening, Andrew," she said, entering the room.

He immediately strode to her and grabbed hold of her hands. "Are you well, Justine?" His eyes swept over her, his expression anxious.

Justine knew that Andrew had been summoned to

Chetsworth Manor, had met with her uncle and father, and had been helping with the inquiries as to who had shot the arrow. But the acute concern on Andrew's face was something Justine had not expected. He looked quite worried as he studied her.

A warm feeling slid through her, from her head to her toes.

"Yes, I am quite well. Besides, we do not know who the arrow was aimed at. It could have been Charlotte—or any one of a number of our friends, including my cousin. Perhaps the marksman had poor aim."

"I can't help thinking it was aimed at you. Or, if not, Charlotte. It would have done more than injure you. The physician your uncle called in identified the substance at the end of the arrow." He hesitated. His hands continued to grip hers, hard.

"What was it?"

"A compound made of the nightshade plant. Belladonna."

Justine gasped softly. "That is highly poisonous." For the first time, a true fear crept along her spine. Her fingers flexed within his warm grasp.

"Yes." He squeezed her hands, studying her, his blue eyes serious.

"But why would someone want to poison me, or Charlotte, or anyone else?"

Andrew let go of her hands, and began to pace. "I don't know." He wore a frown, and as she watched, his face took on a look of grim determination. "But I intend to find out."

Justine's insides softened at the concern in his voice. "Please let me know if you learn of anything." She gripped her hands together, to still their sudden trembling. Suddenly, the intrigues of the novel she was reading seemed all too real.

"Yes, I will." He halted. "In case the arrow was meant for Charlotte, your father and I contacted Kevin too. He is meeting with us on the morrow."

"Well, I am sure you will all get to the bottom of this," Justine said, attempting to make her voice calm. Andrew looked truly perturbed. She glanced at the small clock on the mantle. It was a quarter past the ninth hour. The pendulum swung steadily, the sound almost soothing in its regularity. "I don't suppose you can do anything else tonight."

"No." Andrew stopped, and met her eyes. "But you are to be very careful, Justine. You are not to go anywhere unescorted. Your father and I have agreed on this."

"I don't normally run about unescorted anyway. My father is very proper, as you well know."

"True. But I can't help remembering that I found you on a terrace, two times, quite alone, at two different parties. That will have to stop," he insisted firmly. He folded his arms across his chest.

"Well, really—"

"I am adamant about this. Either I, or your father, shall escort you around at the next party."

Seeing his mind was quite made up, Justine made a decision not to argue the point. She couldn't help the satisfied feeling that encompassed her as he expressed his concerns.

It seemed that Andrew cared for her welfare.

"Well, let us hope that the culprit is caught soon," she murmured.

"Yes." Andrew approached Justine, and as he drew closer, her heart suddenly began that peculiar hammering that it seemed to be doing of late. At least, it did in Andrew's company.

When he was standing right before her, he stopped, and regarded her, his expression still serious.

That somber expression in his eyes had replaced his customary twinkle. He leaned closer, and she could feel his breath on her face.

Their eyes met, and held.

For one heart-stopping second, Justine thought he was going to kiss her again.

Reaching out, Andrew took hold of her right hand and brought it to his lips. His lips were warm as they gently touched her fingers.

He straightened, and his face took on an expression she couldn't decipher.

"Remember to be very careful," he commanded, his voice husky. "I shall take my leave now. I must be out early tomorrow with Edward, continuing our inquiries."

"You be careful too. Good night."

He bowed swiftly, and left.

Justine gazed after him as she heard his footsteps echoing on the marble floor.

Had she imagined Andrew's concern? And was it merely because he knew her, and her family, as friends?

Or was he beginning to feel something more for her?

Something more than friendship—which was precisely, she thought with startling clarity, what she was beginning to feel for him.

* * *

Justine returned to the library, but found she could no longer concentrate on her book. The incident with the arrow seemed to overpower the adventures of the book's characters. She began to walk back and forth, wondering who at the party could have been the target, and why.

As she considered, her mind went back to Andrew. She had never seen such a worried expression on his face. Was it because he cared for her, a little?

She could no longer fool herself. She recognized that she had started to care for Andrew . . . more than she would a mere family friend.

Quite a bit.

No, more than that.

A great deal.

She cared about the way he regarded her. She enjoyed his company. She liked his hands holding hers.

And she liked it when he kissed her.

The door to the library opened suddenly and Charlotte almost bounced into the room.

"Justine!" she cried, her voice full of energy, her mouth smiling widely. "I have just had the most wonderful idea!"

"Oh? What is it?" Justine was glad for the distraction.

Charlotte grabbed Justine's hands, much as Andrew had, and squeezed them. Her blue eyes were fairly dancing.

"If mother and father have no objections, we can have a double wedding!"

Chapter Seven

For a moment, all Justine could do was to stare at her sister. When she finally spoke, she stumbled over her words.

"A . . . *a double wedding?*"

"Yes!" Charlotte was beaming.

Justine's hands felt quite cold compared to Charlotte's warm ones. She drew them away. Her stomach had tightened into a knot, and she sank into the nearest chair.

Things were getting entirely out of hand, she thought dazedly.

"But—Charlotte—"

Charlotte began speaking at the same time. "Then we won't have to wait for you to marry first!"

"Charlotte—remember, mine is not a real engagement!" Justine almost choked out the words.

Charlotte stopped, and gave Justine a knowing look. "Of *course* it is, Justine. I knew you would not become engaged unless you truly wanted to marry. You would never enter into such a false arrangement."

Justine froze. "What did you say?"

"I know you. You might have said you would become engaged to help me. But, then I realized you would never seriously consider the idea unless you truly had feelings for the man and intended to go through with the engagement. I knew when you became engaged to Andrew that you had an affection for him, and it was for real."

Justine thought she was going to fall over. She found herself gripping the edges of the plush red chair.

"Whatever gave you that idea?" Her voice came out like a croaking frog's. "That's not true!"

Charlotte's face took on a serious expression. "Because I know you well. You have not one false bone in your body. I knew that if you became engaged, it was because you truly wanted to marry."

Charlotte stepped over to Justine and, bending down, gave her sister a quick kiss. Her cheek was warm and soft against Justine's cold, stiff one. "I was on the stairs and saw how concerned Andrew was when he arrived. He cares for you as much as you care for him, I am convinced of it! I am truly happy for you, Justine. It is obvious you are falling in love—just like Kevin and I." She straightened, and then ran lightly toward the library door, her skirts swishing.

"But—. Charlotte, you are so much in love that you are assuming that everyone else is in love too!"

Charlotte ignored that comment. "I must go to talk to Mother and Father." Without a backward look, Charlotte hurried from the room.

Justine stared after her sister, still numb with shock.

Had she *really* intended for this to be a pretend engagement?

Justine sprang up, and began to pace the room.

Was Charlotte right? Had she secretly expected to marry Andrew?

Or had she started out pretending . . . and then it had become real?

Or was Charlotte simply imagining everyone felt as in love as she did?

She walked to and fro, the thoughts tumbling together in her mind. Marriage to Andrew . . . a double wedding . . .

Justine let the thought sink into her heart.

And felt an answering yearning.

It was not a thought she shied away from. The idea of marriage to Andrew held definite appeal.

But she knew that, as far as Andrew was concerned, theirs was not a true engagement.

Andrew stared at the clock on the mantle the following evening. Its ticking echoed in the spacious library.

"It seems odd to be here, instead of at Pennington House," Edward said.

"Yes. Whitbury Manor is not home to me yet," Andrew replied. "I was thinking that exact thought before you spoke." He focused on the fireplace, where no fire burned, since the evening was warm.

He had always liked Whitbury Manor. He had moved here since becoming the marquis, but in those few weeks the house, though familiar, was still not his home.

"I will have to keep both homes in good order," he said idly, "and someday my second son will inherit Pennington, while this will go to my first."

"You have to have children before they can inherit," Edward said with a laugh.

There was a moment of silence. Andrew moved from the fireplace and began to pace.

"I have been thinking," he admitted slowly, "how very quiet and empty the house is. It should be filled with revelry, with happy children and adults."

For a moment, Andrew's thoughts hovered on that very idea.

He pictured himself coming home, shedding his hat, and looking up the stairs.

In his mind, Justine ran down to greet him, a smile on her face.

Justine? He was startled to visualize that picture. And to imagine a few shadowy children following at her heels.

Married. To Justine?

The thought and visualizations had a startling appeal. He felt an unaccustomed tugging deep within his soul. A yearning for just such a scenario. A wife, a family . . .

He tried picturing a number of different young women as his wife. Lady Selena Barton, Miss Jane Perthing, Miss Constance Howell, the recently widowed, young Countess of Hartcomer . . .

None held much appeal.

Lady Agatha—he shuddered at that awful thought.

An image of Justine popped into his mind again.

Just thinking about how he had held her several days

before, about how he had lost all thoughts of everything else save her when his lips met hers, he felt a warmth sweep through him.

Edward stood up, breaking Andrew's reverie. "Well, after our fruitless inquiries today, I find I am tired. I will leave so we both may get some rest."

Andrew thought about the inquiries they'd made over the last few days, all to no avail. No one had been able to learn anything about the marksman who had shot the arrow.

It made him more determined than ever to protect Justine. Not that Roderick wouldn't protect his own daughter—it was just that Andrew wanted to keep a constant eye on her.

As Edward was getting ready to take his leave, a knock sounded on the door. "My lord?" It was Jeeson, Andrew's butler from Pennington House.

Jeeson now presided here and Andrew had given old Murray, his uncle's ancient butler, a generous retirement and asked him to recommend a footman to train as butler for Pennington House. Murray had seemed happy to finally retire from his long-held post and return with his wife to his home village. Just yesterday Andrew had received a short note from Murray, thanking him again for the generous stipend which would allow him to live comfortably in a house near his sister's, in a town where his married daughters both resided.

"This just came for you, my lord," Jeeson said, handing Andrew a sealed envelope.

"It is from Roderick Rawlings," Andrew said, drawing out the note. Edward waited, and Andrew quickly read it. He looked up at his friend. "He wants to meet tomorrow to discuss the wedding plans."

Andrew turned to Jeeson. "I will pen a reply in a few minutes which you can give to his footman to take back to Rawlings House."

"Very good." Jeeson gave a bow and left the room.

A sudden vision of Justine, standing on the terrace in the moonlight, appeared in Andrew's mind as he went to pen the letter.

It was late before Justine fell asleep. She kept going over and over the day's events like a pianist practicing scales, until finally, exhausted, she succumbed to slumber. But she awoke at the usual time, and dressing, went down to breakfast.

She found her mother and Charlotte there, and tried to join in the conversation about lace.

"The pieces they had from Belgium were exquisite," Charlotte was saying.

Their mother nodded. "Yes, but there was not much of my favorite design left. Although there were ample lengths of the others . . . I think I will ask if they can try to obtain more."

Justine sipped tea as Charlotte and her mother debated about the kind of lace for Charlotte's white and blue ball gown, the one she was wearing for her official coming out. She asked a question here and there, eating her breakfast slowly.

And then her mother said brightly, "We must soon go to choose a wedding gown for you, Justine."

Justine coughed. "I–I am sure there is plenty of time

before I have to begin looking." She swiftly drank more tea; then bent her head and applied blackberry jam to a scone. The sweet, fruity smell filled her as she tried to breathe slowly and calmly.

"Not as much as one would think," Mary said wisely, pouring more tea. "It is best to look at your leisure, and not be rushed into making such an important decision. It is the most important fashion choice you will make."

Justine swallowed. She cast a glance at Charlotte, who was nodding enthusiastically.

"I shall presently begin to look for mine," Charlotte chirped, like an eager young bird.

Apparently nothing had changed since last night, when Charlotte had convinced herself that Justine wanted to marry Andrew.

Once again, Justine felt that little clutch of fear—or was it excitement?—inside her stomach.

Because she suspected Charlotte was right.

She may have entered this engagement with the intention of it being a pretense for Charlotte's sake— and for the sake of getting Andrew some peace and quiet—but the idea of marrying Andrew was starting to hold appeal.

What would it be like, she wondered dreamily, being Andrew's wife? The pluses of being married to a titled man might be nice, but she had never felt they were essential. Her father was untitled yet her mother and their entire family led happy lives. She had always wanted to simply be comfortable, with someone she liked and respected.

And she liked Andrew. He was amusing, and considerate of others. And she respected him for his intelligence and loyalty to his family and friends.

Of course, he could be a terrible tease—but did not every man have his flaws? He was not a spendthrift, or a liar, or overly fond of the gaming tables. He seemed more thoughtful than many suitors she had met.

For one moment, she imagined him returning home after a day spent checking on his estates, pulling her into his arms, and kissing her as he had the other night.

He would indeed make a good husband, she knew.

For someone else.

The thought was like cold water dashed on her face.

"Justine? Justine! I am speaking to you."

Her mother's tone broke into her thoughts like lightning forking through clouds.

"Oh! I am sorry. I was daydreaming about . . . about marriage," she said hastily, her cheeks warming.

Her mother smiled indulgently. "As well you should, dear. Now is the time to dream and prepare."

Justine bent her head, knowing her cheeks must be quite pink, and inhaled the familiar aroma of tea with honey. But not before she had caught a glimpse of Charlotte's beaming face.

Oh dear, now Charlotte would be more convinced than ever that Justine truly did want to marry Andrew.

He *would* make a most suitable husband, a little voice inside her said.

She was pondering this thought and trying to ignore Charlotte's infectious grin when a servant entered.

"Mr. Rawlings requests the presence of his daughters' company following breakfast," he intoned.

Justine looked in surprise to their mother, who was nodding.

"Yes." Seeing Justine's questioning look, she said, "As soon as you girls finish your breakfast, you may be excused. Your father has something to discuss with you."

Uneasily Justine finished off the scone and wiped her fingers on the linen napkin. Seeing that Charlotte was finishing her juice, she rose, and Charlotte followed.

"We will see you later, Mother," Charlotte said, looking cheerful. In fact, since Father had said Charlotte could marry Kevin, it seemed to Justine that her sister forever wore a smile on her face.

Their mother smiled as they left the room.

"Do you know what this is about?" Justine whispered to Charlotte as they walked down the corridor and turned to the wing where Father's study was located.

Charlotte nodded. "I believe it has something to do with my idea last night."

Justine fell silent, her nerves tightening.

When they knocked on the study door, their father bid them to enter. Justine opened the door, and found to her surprise that Andrew and Kevin sat in chairs in front of Father's desk.

The two young men leaped up at the same time, offering their chairs to the sisters.

Justine bit her lip, casting an uncertain glance at Andrew. He gave her a friendly smile. What on earth was he going to think if Charlotte was right and Father wanted to discuss the idea of a double wedding? Justine took her seat, smoothing out the skirt of her white-and-green-striped gown. Her hands felt damp against the cool material.

Roderick had also stood up. Now he smiled at his daughters.

"My two eldest daughters," he said proudly. "I am most fortunate. Not only are you two wonderful daughters, but you have chosen to marry commendable men." He paused to send approving smiles to both Andrew and Kevin.

"Men from good, noble families. And men who will take good care of you. I have carefully observed both of them in the past several days. No two young men could have tried more diligently to find the person who shot the arrow." A shadow passed over his face. "However, that is not why we are here today. Let us focus on more positive events.

"I have summoned Andrew and Kevin here today to discuss your idea, daughters, of having a double wedding."

Justine felt her whole body stiffen. Their idea? She sent Charlotte an accusing look, but her sister was innocently smiling at their father. Charlotte must have told Father this was Justine's idea as well—or that Justine had agreed to it. Before she could say anything, Father went on.

"Both Andrew and Kevin have no objections to the idea of a double wedding," Father said. "In fact, they favor it." He looked at both young men, who nodded.

Justine had to swallow a gasp.

"It means, Charlotte, that you and Kevin can marry sooner," Father said. Kevin smiled widely at the words, and reached over to clasp Charlotte's hand. Charlotte was positively glowing.

"And Justine," Roderick continued, "you may recall, Andrew's sisters married in a double ceremony, and so did his mother and her own sister. It is almost a family custom." He glanced at Andrew, who also smiled, and moved to place a hand on Justine's shoulder in a gesture she found strangely reassuring. His hand warmed her through the thin material of her dress. Without thinking, she reached out and grasped it with her own, and hung on.

She had forgotten about his sisters' double ceremony. But *how* could he agree to this? Her thoughts whirled around in her head. A double wedding? Charlotte and Kevin, Andrew and herself?

Of course, if they planned a double wedding, and then Justine broke her engagement, it would leave Charlotte and Kevin free to marry soon. Which was the purpose of Justine's false engagement, after all. That and to keep away the many women pursuing Andrew—

"But what about . . . Andrew's mourning period?" she asked, her voice coming out raspy. Her stomach had tightened.

Andrew stepped back, releasing her hand. "My period of mourning need not be protracted. It was my uncle and cousin who died, not an immediate family member."

Stunned, Justine was uncertain of what else to say, only semi-conscious of the conversation from the others. She heard Kevin say something to Charlotte, then Andrew again. At his voice, she snapped back to attention.

". . . plan the guest list for my side of the family with the help of Mrs. Rawlings and my sisters, since my own mother is gone," Andrew was saying.

The guest list? *The guest list?*

"On our side, it should be simple enough to plan one big wedding instead of two," Roderick replied. "Of course my wife will be eager to help you in any way she can. Your mother, Claire, would have done the same if the situation was reversed. Mary has already spoken to me of this. She is most astute at making arrangements and seeing them through. And Kevin's mother will be happy to help too, I am certain."

"I am grateful," Andrew said emphatically.

"This is a splendid plan," Roderick finished. "Now, I will seek out Mary and we shall begin preparations. And Kevin, I will send a note round to your father asking him to meet with me later. I believe he is back in London?"

"Yes, he arrived yesterday from our estate," Kevin said eagerly.

Roderick nodded, a satisfied smile on his face. "Very good." He walked over to his daughters, bent and kissed first Justine, then Charlotte. "My dears. I am most happy." He inclined his head to Andrew and Kevin. "I will see you both soon." And he left his study with a firm step and a smile on his face.

Charlotte grabbed at Kevin's hand again. "Oh, Kevin!"

"We shall be married soon!" Kevin declared, a look of supreme happiness covering his face.

Justine turned to look at Andrew, knowing her confusion must be apparent. She saw understanding in his face, and he bent to take her hand firmly in his.

"Let us go for a walk," he said quietly, "so we may both have a few moments to ourselves."

Gratefully, she let him pull her to her feet and lead her out of the room. As they left, she saw Kevin pulling Charlotte into his arms.

Andrew led the way to the nearest door to the garden. He indicated a bench in the shade of a tree.

Justine could not sit down; she was too agitated. She walked over to a rose bush and bent her head to inhale its fragrance. A breeze stirred the bush, but the air outside was already warm. It would be a hot day.

She turned to find Andrew studying her.

"I tried to discourage Charlotte from this idea," Justine began, her voice unsteady. "I was afraid things would get out of hand, when she suggested it last night. And it appears that is exactly what is happening. I am so sorry. I had no idea my father would embrace the idea."

"That is fine," Andrew said quietly, stepping closer. "It is actually in keeping with your plans to let Charlotte marry Kevin."

"I know, but—" Justine stopped. What more could she say? "It seems we are digging ourselves into a deeper hole. It is going to be harder to . . . extricate ourselves . . . from this engagement."

"I know." Yet Andrew didn't seem particularly perturbed by the fact. If anything, he looked slightly amused. Justine gritted her teeth. Was everything amusing to him?

After a moment, his expression became more serious, and he said, "Did you not want a realistic engagement, Justine? This will certainly be in keeping with one. Your sister can make her plans, and when the time is right, you will end our engagement. And then I am positive your parents will let Charlotte and Kevin go ahead, since they will be in the throes of wedding plans."

"Yes, they probably will. You are right, it will look completely realistic."

"And in the meantime," he continued, almost jovially, "you can study the other gentlemen out there who are searching for wives, and decide who catches your fancy. And I will have a nice reprieve from the marriage-minded set, until I, too, am ready."

As Justine regarded Andrew, she found her chest tightening. Why did the thought of looking for a husband among the ton hold little appeal? And the idea of Andrew someday looking in earnest for a bride—that thought was even more distasteful.

Andrew had drawn closer. His eyes once again took on a devilish spark. "I see your sisters are regarding us from an upstairs window. No, don't look. Remember, Justine, we must act as if this engagement is real." He bent down and, touched his lips to hers.

Once again his kiss created a bevy of sensations. She grew quite warm, feeling as if she was floating. His lips pressed harder this time. She wanted this kiss despite their pretense. Her hands surrounded his neck as if of their own accord, and she found herself clinging to Andrew. His embrace grew tighter.

Girlish laughter pealed through the open window.

Andrew let her go and stepped back.

Justine regarded him, fighting to catch her breath. That was the kind of kiss the poets wrote of, she thought, somewhat dazed by its intensity. Seeking to get her balance back, she looked up, and caught sight of Ginette and Arabella, ogling them. The minute her young sisters saw Justine regarding them, they scampered away from the window.

She turned to look at Andrew.

Andrew's expression was almost surprised, and as she watched him, it changed—to something more guarded.

"I will take my leave now," he said, and his voice sounded somewhat stiff. "I shall return this evening and let your father know if there is any news from my inquiries."

"I will see you then," Justine said, her voice coming out breathlessly.

This time, he took the tips of her fingers and brushed the merest kiss on them. With a serious nod, he left her.

Justine sank down on the stone bench, and touched her lips with trembling fingers. Her lips were still hot from Andrew's kiss.

Lord, if this was a kiss one gave a fake fiancée, what kind of kiss would Andrew give to a real intended?

Justine felt a yearning to find out.

Chapter Eight

Andrew stood in the ballroom at Count Seyling's mansion, Edward on one side and Justine, Charlotte and Kevin on his other. Stringed instruments played harmoniously while glittering lords and ladies walked on the outskirts of the room, talking and laughing. In the center, many danced. The ball was in full swing and the mild May evening, with just a touch of mist, had brought the ton out in force for the count's annual, lavish ball.

Justine looked beautiful in a dress of deep rose, and was speaking to her sister, who was dressed in pale blue. Andrew's eyes kept returning to Justine, though he was listening to an amusing story Edward was relaying about the Earl of Bradbury.

Justine looked like a princess tonight. Her dark hair, swept up on her head, shone like satin. Her complexion was creamy and glowed in the light of hundreds of candles. Her dark eyes sparkled, and Andrew was certain that, had she not been engaged, every young buck there would be following her and begging her for a dance.

As it was, many, many people had stopped to wish them well on their coming nuptials. Andrew had been both amused and relieved, realizing he no longer had to avoid all the marriageable young women and their persistent mothers.

And yet, he had another, strange feeling too. One he could not quite put a finger on.

Lord and Lady Fornay wished them well, then moved past them to be replaced by their friends Sir and Lady Chanders. Justine spoke to Lady Chanders, then caught Andrew's eye. She smiled up at him.

Something tightened in his chest and he smiled back.

For several days, ever since their kiss in the garden, Justine had been on his mind almost constantly. The kiss had replayed itself in his head a hundred times. What had started out as a playful kiss had become all too real, catching fire, and threatening to burn him.

He had kissed other women before. But he had never had a reaction like that to any other kiss. As if he'd touched fire, and was about to be singed!

He was abruptly brought back to the present by the warm smile of Lady Chanders. After expressing their felicitations, the Chanders followed their friends the Fornays, and Lady Agatha and her mother approached. Andrew forced himself to smile.

". . . wishing you well, m'lord," the heavy woman said somewhat stiffly. He caught Lady Agatha giving Justine a sullen glance.

Justine met her look head on, and regally nodded her head and gave the young woman a small smile. He saw

Agatha's cheeks redden, and she moved past with a murmur.

He was glad Justine was not intimidated by the jealous women there tonight. Not that she had any worries. Not one of them could hold a candle to her. Justine's inner and outer beauty was unsurpassed.

He couldn't imagine staying in Lady Agatha's presence for more than five minutes. He watched as the young woman sent Charlotte an equally baleful glance. Apparently Lady Agatha, the daughter of an earl, was not happy to see women younger than herself making estimable matches.

Kevin's and Charlotte's engagement had not yet been announced, but rumors were flying that night that it was imminent, Edward had told him. Certainly, looking at Kevin as he gazed at Charlotte's pretty face, it was evident that he was besotted.

The music paused, and Andrew saw Justine glance over toward the orchestra.

"Would you care to dance?" he asked her, bending closer.

"Oh, yes," she replied, her smile lighting up her face.

He bowed, then took her hand and escorted her onto the dance floor.

The musicians began playing, and Andrew took hold of Justine and swung her into the dance. She was light on her feet and graceful, and it felt good as they glided through the steps together. Very good, he thought.

They stepped around the room in perfect unison. He caught sight of Roderick and Mary Rawlings smiling fondly at them, then Edward's brother Lawrence, who raised a glass to them.

They turned, moving smoothly around the floor, passing by Charlotte and Kevin, then by Henry and a young woman who Andrew didn't recognize.

He glanced down at Justine, and found that she was gazing at him. She looked lovely, but he could not read the expression on her face. She appeared . . . thoughtful, perhaps.

He usually simply tolerated dancing, but dancing with her was a surprising treat. Their hands touching, their steps matching, Justine fit perfectly in the loose embrace that the dance called for.

She tilted her head further and smiled suddenly as she gracefully circled him.

He smiled back, and for a moment the sounds of the ball, the music, the laughter, all seemed to fade into the distance.

And he had the absurd desire to kiss her, right there, in the middle of the ballroom.

He restrained himself, but with a surprising effort. What was wrong with him? To have a desire to kiss his supposed fiancé in public? He must be overwrought, he thought, to be having such impulses.

Or perhaps he simply wanted to relive their intense kiss of the other day.

The dance ended, and he gave her a bow. Justine's color was high.

"Did you enjoy that, my dear?" he asked somewhat formally, striving to hide his unaccustomed emotional state.

"Yes," she answered simply.

He realized he still had hold of her hand. He was

unsure why he was acting so oddly. Perhaps he could use some male companionship, he thought.

"I will leave you with your parents," he said. "I promised Edward I would consult with him on something."

"Of course," she agreed after a second.

He led her towards Roderick and Mary, who were conversing with Kevin's parents and the dowager Duchess of Clearfield, a sharp-eyed lady if ever there was one.

As they drew close, Isobel Newmont stepped into their path. She looked lovely in a white and silver gown, yet she reminded Andrew of nothing so much as a column of ice.

"My lord." Her tone was just as cold as her appearance. She acknowledged Justine with a nod of her head. "Congratulations on your upcoming marriage."

"Thank you," Andrew said, and which Justine echoed in a firm voice.

Isobel turned slightly to look at Justine. Andrew glanced at Justine, who met Isobel's look with an unwavering one. He turned back to Isobel to catch a full-fledged glare on her face.

In an instant, the expression was gone, replaced by a bland one as Isobel moved away. But he had seen the venom in Isobel's icy countenance. It was enough to make a person recoil.

Roderick's oldest brother, the Earl of Denton, and his wife approached. Andrew had met them at Charlotte's coming out ball last week and now listened to their comments about how delighted they were with their niece's betrothal. They were soon joined by

Justine's uncle, the Earl of Chetsworth, and his wife, Mary's sister; and it was easy for Andrew to make his excuses to Justine. She was well chaperoned by her many family members.

"I will return later," he told her. "I promised Edward I would speak to him," he repeated. Edward had declared he'd like to spend some time at the card tables, and Andrew needed to get away from the increasingly warm ballroom, and from the strange sensations that had enveloped him as Justine swayed in his arms to the music.

Justine tried to quell her disappointment as Andrew disappeared into the crowd. Of course men rarely spent the entire evenings beside their fiancés or wives, she was well aware. Doing so might even make people suspicious of their "engagement." Yet she had hoped to be with him for a longer period after the romantic dance they had shared.

Dancing in Andrew's arms to the beat of splendid music had been terribly exciting. Justine felt as if she'd been transported to the clouds and was dancing on divine air.

She sighed, and caught Charlotte's eye.

Charlotte smiled, and Justine wondered if Charlotte's idea that Justine was sweet on Andrew was actually causing her to feel that very way.

"There is such a crush here," Adelaide, her cousin, said from next to her. "I vow every member of the ton is here tonight."

"Not quite," her brother remarked, "but many . . . ah, there is Selena. Excuse me," he said, and went towards Justine's friend.

Justine and Adelaide grinned at each other, and then, seeing a young man approaching her cousin, Justine excused herself to go to the retiring room, thinking to leave them alone.

Besides, she could use a few moments to herself. Moments in which to relive the excitement of dancing with Andrew, of being held by him.

She managed to elude notice. Her parents had followed her and Charlotte so much the last few days she was glad of the crowded ball, which they must deem a safe place.

Even in the retiring room, the crowd was thick. Sitting before a mirror and checking her hair, Justine found herself already wondering how soon she would see Andrew again.

Someone sat on a chair near her, and she paid little attention, until she heard the whiny voice.

Lady Agatha.

". . . of course, I am certain he is marrying her because their families have known each other for ages . . . what other reason could there be?" she was saying in a snide voice to the young woman beside her. "Her father has no title, although his family is an old one. But perhaps it is her money . . ."

In the mirror, Justine saw color flood her cheeks at Agatha's unkind words. It was obvious Agatha knew she was right there and was intentionally speaking loudly.

Justine held her tongue. She certainly did not want to start an altercation with the nasty woman, even if she could think of a smart retort. She picked up her fan and waved it in front of her warm face.

The young woman beside Agatha said something in a low voice that Justine couldn't hear, and Agatha chuckled. Then Agatha continued, "And that sister of hers . . . I hear tell she is to marry a country bumpkin . . . well, perhaps she can do no better."

It was one thing to insult her, but to insult her sister—that was quite enough! Justine snapped her fan closed with a loud report.

"I would not make such harsh comments if I were you," she said in a voice more strident than her ordinary one. "People might get the idea, Lady Agatha, that you are a sharp-tongued vixen. Or perhaps they think that already?" She smiled briefly, conscious that her lips trembled. "Which may explain why there are no beaux surrounding you this evening."

The room had fallen mostly silent, and several women tittered at Justine's words. Agatha had turned to stare at her, and her face grew an intense red color. She opened her mouth to speak.

"Well said, my dear," the dowager Duchess of Clearfield stated. Justine started. She hadn't realized the older woman stood behind her, just out of view. The duchess turned to look hard at Agatha. "You must learn, young woman, when to keep your thoughts to yourself. Now, I suggest you return to your mother. She will have the good sense to tell you that one should not deliberately anger the future wife of a marquis. Or a duchess like myself," she finished wryly.

Gratitude at the duchess' championship swept through Justine—and just a little pride that she herself had spoken up to the nasty Agatha. Agatha stood, looking suddenly close to tears, and practically ran from the room, the young woman next to her following in her wake.

The duchess sat next to Justine as whispers and giggles began to fly through the room. "That should put her in her place," she told Justine. "My word, Fredricka has let that young lady get quite out of hand. I believe I shall have a word with her."

"Thank you," Justine murmured quietly.

"Not at all. You handled it well, my dear, I just gave it a little more punch." The duchess gave her regal smile. "You are quite a clever young lady—and loyal to your dear sister. It is no wonder Andrew is head over heels."

Head over heels?

A sudden emotion surged through Justine at the duchess' words. She probed the feeling, and recognized it as hope.

Could the duchess be right? Did Andrew care?

Justine hastened to complete her toilette, eager to find Andrew. She went to the room's door with the duchess, and on her way out several young women congratulated her on putting Agatha in her place.

"I wish I had done so," one woman, older than Justine, said fervently.

But as they left the room, one woman stepped from a corner.

Isobel.

And she was staring at Justine with eyes full of resentment.

Justine was taken aback. Her heart was still hammering from the encounter with Agatha, and she met Isobel's look head on. Isobel turned away, bending to check the skirt of her gown, and avoided Justine's look. But a pulse of trepidation rushed through Justine.

Isobel's look had been positively malevolent. Worse than Lady Agatha's.

Justine forced herself to hold her head high as she accompanied the duchess back to the ballroom.

Within five minutes, Jane rushed up to her.

"Justine," she whispered, "word has it that you and Lady Agatha had words . . . and that you put her in her place!" Her eyes gleamed.

Charlotte and Adelaide had joined them. "Do tell," Adelaide urged. "Why, Sir Montell's eldest daughter said she was beside herself, trying not to laugh, but that Agatha got what she well deserved."

Rather embarrassed, Justine related the story. Charlotte gasped indignantly at Agatha's words. Their mother joined them, and did not say a word, but Justine had a feeling that Mary, too, had already heard the gossip—and with her serene smile was letting Justine know she thought she had handled herself well. Perhaps the duchess had even said so. Undoubtedly, Mary would have something to say about it in private.

Later, by the time Andrew and Edward had found their group, Justine was afraid the story had become somewhat exaggerated.

Andrew handed her a glass of lemonade.

"I hear tell, Justine," he began in his teasing voice, "that a certain young lady verbally sparred with Lady Agatha Rembody." Laughter lit his eyes. "And that she very cleverly stopped Lady Agatha from scathing remarks toward the young lady's sister." He raised his own glass. "Have you any idea who this paragon is?"

"You need not tease, Andrew," Justine said, sipping the refreshing drink. "It was myself. And, I only did it when she made remarks about Charlotte. I did repress comments when she spoke about me."

"Very commendable." He laughed. "You are a loyal sibling, to be sure. I admire your ability to stand up to Lady Agatha. There are few more disagreeable than her."

The incident was rather amusing, Justine had to admit to herself later, during the carriage ride home. Almost amusing enough to wipe away the memory of Isobel's terrible glare.

Agatha might have been nasty. But Isobel was full of hatred, and truly made Justine feel uneasy.

Chapter Nine

" . . . And Eleanor told me that her mother said that Lady Fredricka Rembody packed her daughter Agatha off and sent her to visit her aunt in Scotland for a month!" Charlotte declared as their carriage rolled through the streets of London. They had met her friend Eleanor on Bond Street while visiting the dressmaker.

Mary nodded to her two oldest daughters. "Yes, Frances, the Duchess of Clearfield told me she was going to suggest that. She felt Agatha needed to reflect on her own behavior." Mary smiled. "Few would argue with the duchess."

"Reflect? It sounds more like punishment to me," Charlotte said.

"Well, that particular aunt is very strict," Mary conceded.

"Perhaps she will come back with a new perspective," Justine said dryly. "Or at least a more civil tongue."

Charlotte giggled.

"And Eleanor was saying," Charlotte continued, "how envious our friends are that I am making a love match! They are saying that Kevin has loved me since we were but little children, and could look at no other!"

Justine gazed out at the stately manor they were passing, barely seeing the gray stone walls. It had been an enjoyable excursion, but now she was glad they were heading home. She needed time to think, away from Mama's prying eyes and Charlotte's constant, bright prattle.

It was one week since the Seyling ball, and they had spent the better part of the day selecting dresses and accessories for their trousseaus. While Justine had delighted in choosing from among the beautiful fabrics and latest styles of gowns, the day had been a sharp reminder that she was falsely engaged. She was feeling not only guilty about her new wardrobe; she felt surprisingly wistful too.

Justine had tried to persuade her mother not to buy so many clothes for her. Mary had looked at her askance; and in order to avoid her mother's suspicions, Justine had dropped the idea.

Yet, she couldn't help wishing that she could enjoy this shopping as much as her sister. Wishing that she was a bride who was truly picking out her trousseau.

"Eleanor was saying you, Justine, are the absolute envy of every young lady amongst the ton," Charlotte continued merrily. "Marrying a marquis! The most eligible and handsome bachelor of the season!" She beamed as Justine refocused her attention on her. Obviously, Charlotte was happy in her choice, and not at all envious.

Their carriage rolled to a stop in front of Rawlings.

"You girls go in and get some rest," Mary said, as a footman appeared to help them out. "I will return home after my meeting with the baker."

"Please bring home the sketches for the wedding cake," Charlotte requested as she alighted.

"I will indeed," their mother promised.

Justine exited the carriage next. Charlotte walked with Justine up the stairs, into the cool hall, yawning.

"I am fatigued," she said. "Shopping is so exciting, but I think I will lie down now."

"Go ahead," Justine urged. "I'm going to sit in the library and read. I am too restless right now to nap."

Charlotte gave Justine a happy smile before running lightly up the stairs. Justine stared after her for a moment.

She pulled listlessly at her gloves, feeling the soft fabric against her warm hands. Somewhere upstairs she heard George's young, jovial voice, then Charlotte's. Faintly, she heard voices from the kitchen wing, the servants chattering and laughing. It was too early for dinner preparations, and she guessed they were sitting down for a pot of tea and gossip.

Two footmen were still carrying in some of their purchases, the ones that didn't have to be custom made. Looking at the parcels containing gloves and fans and other accessories, Justine decided to unpack later. She would follow her original plan and go to her favorite room, the library, where she could relax and read.

"May I get you anything, Miss Justine?" Their butler, as always, seemed to read her mind.

"Thank you, Danvers. Some tea in the library would be most welcome."

"Certainly. I'll have it prepared at once."

Justine walked over to the library. With her father gone to supervise one of his land holdings, this wing of the house was quiet.

Light shone through the windows into the red and gold library, but the afternoon sun was stronger in another wing, so here it was not so warm.

Justine dropped her gloves on a table and went to search out something to read. She wanted something light and lively, something that would take her mind off her troubled thoughts.

She found herself drawn to one of her favorite volumes, *Twelfth Night* by William Shakespeare. Within minutes Justine was happily ensconced in her favorite chair, immersing herself in Mr. Shakespeare's madcap comedy.

A timid knock on the door startled her. Her tea. Justine called out, and the new maid, a young girl, probably only fifteen or sixteen, entered.

"Your tea, Miss Justine," the girl said. Her voice was nervous.

"You may leave it on the table there," Justine murmured. As Justine watched the girl pour tea into the blue china cup, she noted the girl's hand was actually trembling. The silver teapot clinked against the china.

Poor thing, she was new and nervous. Justine smiled kindly at her. "Thank you, Celia."

"Do you need anything else?" The young woman clutched her hands.

"No, I will add sugar myself. And thank cook for her biscuits." Justine noted the neat pile of her favorites on the accompanying plate. She smiled. "That will be all, Celia. Thank you."

The girl gave an awkward curtsy and hurriedly left.

Justine added sugar to her tea, stirring, and sipped it when it cooled. Then she immersed herself once more in the antics of Viola and Sebastian.

The characters' amusing escapades caught her up in the play, and it wasn't until she heard the clock on the mantle chime three that she realized how completely absorbed she had been. She put her book down, feeling better. Somehow reading always helped her look at things with a more positive perspective.

She poured more tea, which was now delightfully cool, and added sugar. The fragrant brew was invigorating. Munching on cook's special biscuits, she thought about Andrew.

She sighed, and was about to refocus her attention on Viola and Sebastian when she heard a noise outside the library door.

It sounded like someone crying.

Justine set her cup down carefully, listening.

There it was again. A sob.

She sprang up. Was it Charlotte? What could be wrong? She'd been so happy just an hour ago—

Justine moved quickly to the door, and opened it.

"Charlotte?" she asked, entering the shadowy hall.

A movement to her right caught her eye. Justine turned, in time to see a dark–clothed figure wielding a candlestick.

She cried out, and sprang back as the candlestick came towards her.

But she didn't move as fast as the dark figure.

There was a pain at the side of her head. She felt herself falling into blackness . . .

Chapter Ten

"You had some concerns you wanted to share with me?" Roderick began without preamble as he took a seat next to Andrew at Green's Gentleman's Club.

"Yes, sir. Shall I ring for a brandy?"

Roderick waved his hand. "Perhaps later. Tell me what is on your mind, Andrew."

Andrew hesitated for a moment. He had just come from another visit to one of the Whitbury estates with his business manager, and had partaken in a lively discussion about the improvements he wanted to make. But all through his visit, worries about Justine and her safety had poked at him. By noon he had determined to meet with Roderick, and promptly sent a note around to request the meeting. Roderick, returning from a visit to one of his own estates, had replied that he would meet him in the afternoon.

"I have some concerns about Justine's safety," Andrew reiterated slowly. "And Charlotte's as well. But

I thought I would speak to you before involving Kevin. I want to be sure I am not overreacting."

"'Tis better to err on the side of caution where my daughters are concerned," Roderick stated. "What is your concern?"

Briefly, Andrew told Roderick that he was worried, since they had been unable to learn anything further about the person who had shot the arrow. "I fear the perpetrator may attempt this again. We must do everything possible to safeguard your daughters."

Roderick nodded in assent. "Of course. I ordered an extra servant to accompany them whenever they leave the house, right after the incident. And for my wife and other children as well. I have also hired additional help, which is especially important, since my youngest girls returned from the country, and Walter returns from Eton this day."

"Thank you," Andrew said gravely. He did not add that he, and his friend Edward, had discussed the situation thoroughly again, only the day before. They suspected that if someone meant to harm Justine, it was because they wanted to eliminate her as Andrew's future wife. In other words, the path to marriage with a marquis would be clear again.

Roderick was an astute man. "There is one possible motive that has occurred to me, a motive that someone could have for harming Justine." He learned forward in his chair, his expression grim, and lowered his voice. "If they hoped that with my daughter out of the way— the good Lord protect us—then the way would be clear for someone else to marry you—that could be a motive. Someone who is desperate to have a daughter marry you, perhaps, or a sister—"

"Mr. Rawlings! Mr. Rawlings!" The voice of a breathless footman echoed from down the hall.

"In the Gold Room," someone responded as Roderick sat up straight.

"In here," he called out, frowning.

Andrew looked anxiously at the footman who rushed toward them. The young man appeared upset, and Andrew immediately tensed. Was something wrong? Justine—

"What is it, Harridan?" Roderick asked.

"Sir, there is an emergency at Rawlings. George sent me to fetch you."

Both Andrew and Roderick jumped to their feet at the words.

"What kind of emergency?" Roderick demanded.

Andrew was already moving toward the door. "We'll come at once."

"It's Miss Justine, sir." The footman gasped for breath. "George says she has been assaulted with a candlestick."

"Assaulted!" Andrew thought for a moment his heart had stopped. "Is she—is she—" He couldn't get the words out.

"Is she well?" Roderick barked, gripping the chair next to him. "Is my daughter unharmed?"

"She appears to be injured. They've sent for the doctor."

Cold fear struck Andrew like the harshest winter wind.

Andrew and Roderick exchanged a swift, horrified glance before springing into action.

Andrew ran down the hall, Roderick at his heels.

* * *

The usual quiet, composed atmosphere at Rawlings was gone. In its place was a feeling of anxiety. Servants scurried about nervously, their expressions worried, their tones low.

By the time Andrew and Roderick reached the house, Mary had returned and was in the library with Justine and the physician. Danvers filled Roderick and Andrew in on the details as they hurried down the halls to the library.

Charlotte stood outside the room, leaning against her younger brother George, as they spoke to the housekeeper. George was subdued, his usual lively countenance serious, and Charlotte's eyes were brimming with tears. The housekeeper was speaking quietly to both of them in a soothing voice.

". . . sure she'll be fine," she said.

"How is she?" Roderick asked as he rushed forward.

"Mrs. Rawlings and the doctor are in with her now. It appears she has a wound on her head, but she was able to talk when I had her carried to the sofa."

Roderick nodded, his face all concern for his oldest child. He knocked loudly at the door. "Mary. May I come in?"

Mary's voice bid him to enter, and he disappeared inside. Andrew started to follow until he heard Roderick's voice. "Wait here. I will tell you as soon as you may enter."

Andrew gripped his hands. He was most anxious to see Justine with his own eyes, to ascertain if she was well, and to be told to wait . . . ! He had to force himself not to barge into the room.

The housekeeper leaned forward. "I'm sure you may see her in a few minutes, my lord. The doctor is probably nearly done with examining her."

He knew it would be unseemly for him to be in the room with his fiancé during the doctor's visit, but damn, he wanted to see if she was unharmed, to see her with his own eyes! He began to pace.

The fear that had encompassed him since the footman's announcement was growing. He had not felt anything like this turmoil since the day he learned his parents had perished. He had to restrain himself from wringing his hands. Instead, he folded them across his chest.

He came to a halt beside George and Charlotte. "What happened?" he demanded.

George spoke first. "I was playing outside, when I saw a person come dashing out of the side door, near the rose garden. He had all dark clothes and a mask— I knew no one dressed like that had any business in the house! I yelled after him, but he ran fast and disappeared. I started to follow, but I had this feeling . . . I don't know, like I should check on things inside the house." His grave voice took on a note of youthful importance. "It is my home, and I wanted to see if something was amiss—the very way the man ran, made me suspicious—"

"Yes?" Andrew asked anxiously, striving to hold his patience. George was no more than twelve; it was commendable that he had the presence of mind to see if there was something wrong, and to summon help. Andrew tried to sound more appreciative. "You did well to check the house, and to summon your father when you knew something was wrong."

George stood up straighter, and his voice became stronger. "When I went in, I saw Justine lying on the floor. The side of her head was bruised, and I was scared. But after a minute I saw she was breathing, and I called for help."

George went on to describe how the servants rushed over to Justine. He had asked Danvers to summon his father, and their physician. His chest puffed slightly as he recalled making the decisions as the temporary man of the house.

"And the noise roused Charlotte from her nap," George continued.

"I had them carry Justine to the couch," Charlotte said, her voice tremulous. "And thank goodness, Mama returned just then." She hugged her brother.

"And she asked Danvers to start questioning everyone," George added.

"You handled things well," Andrew praised. He resumed his pacing. "Pray God she is in good health."

"She said her head hurt," Charlotte said, "but nothing else did."

"To think of this happening here," murmured the housekeeper, who was clutching her hands, "at Rawlings."

"How did the assailant get in?" Andrew asked sharply.

The woman bit her lip. "Danvers discovered the side door by the rose garden was unlatched. He believes the man may have entered and left that way."

"I myself left the house by the kitchen door," George

said. "That is where I usually come and go when I'm playing outside."

"Did any of the servants notice anything amiss?" Andrew asked. Doing something, even questioning, was better than standing here helplessly.

"Cook discovered a short time ago that one of the servants has disappeared," the housekeeper said, frowning.

Charlotte gasped and Andrew repeated sharply, "Disappeared? Who disappeared?"

"The new girl, Celia. No one has seen her since cook sent Miss Justine her tea."

That did not bode well for the new serving girl. "What do you know of her?" His voice remained sharp.

"Has someone abducted her?" Charlotte asked, her face even paler.

George's eyes widened.

"We know very little, my lord. She was hired only last week when Marie married and left to join her husband at the Rawlings' country estate. The girl did have references," the housekeeper said.

"Did you check these references?" Andrew tried to calm his voice. He did not mean to give the housekeeper any grief, but he had to do something, anything.

"Of course." The woman's mouth became a thin line. "One was from Lady Overbridge's housekeeper. She had known Celia's family for years. They are destitute and Celia needed a job badly, she said."

Andrew softened his voice. "I'm sorry. I did not mean to imply you hadn't checked on her. It is just that, in this situation, we must investigate everything." He paused a moment as the woman visibly relaxed. "A very poor girl might be bribed, perhaps, to leave the door open . . ."

At that moment, the library door opened, and Roderick appeared.

"She will be all right," he said, his voice full of relief. "You may all come in."

Andrew was the first in the room, followed by Charlotte and George, and the housekeeper.

The doctor and Mary were standing beside the couch, where Justine sat propped up by pillows. Her hair was pulled back from the left side of her face, and a dark bruise was evident there.

Andrew's heart constricted at the sight of her injury, and anger at the man who had done this boiled within him.

"I am fine," Justine declared in a reassuring voice as they all gathered by the sofa. "Except for the headache."

Without thinking, Andrew took her hands in his. They were starkly cold. He studied her pale but composed face.

She was being brave, he decided. Her head must be throbbing.

"Are you sure?" Worry gnawed at his insides.

She smiled briefly. "Yes."

"She must rest for several days," the physician said. "Fortunately, the injury is not so bad, and is on the side of her head."

"Father, I want to tell you what I saw," Justine said.

Andrew looked down at her anxiously. Her beautiful face might be pale, but her expression was determined. He glanced at Roderick.

"Very well," her father said. "As briefly as possible, so we may catch this culprit. I intend to send for the Bow Street runners."

Justine described hearing someone cry, and how, when she left the library, the darkly clothed figure had been there with the candlestick.

"And I jumped out of the way but I was not quick enough. I saw the candlestick coming toward me, but that's all that I remember." She winced.

"Don't think about it anymore," Andrew instructed, squeezing her soft hands. They were still icy, and it was obvious Justine was in pain. He chafed her hands, hoping to warm them. "We will catch the dastardly culprit," he added, his voice filled with determination.

"Why would someone strike you?" George's innocent question was full of youthful curiosity.

There was silence. Andrew was afraid he could guess why.

"We're going to find out." Roderick's voice sounded grim.

"And when we do, he will be dealt with. Swiftly," Andrew promised.

He turned to Roderick. "Your housekeeper tells me one of the maids is missing. It may have something to do with this."

Justine and Mary both gasped, and Roderick said, "Missing?" He turned to the housekeeper. "Mrs. Conroy, who is missing?"

"The new girl, Celia," the housekeeper said, wringing her hands.

Justine made a sound. "Oh dear. I wondered why she was so nervous."

"What do you mean?" Roderick questioned, leaning toward his daughter.

Justine described how unusually nervous the new maid had seemed, how her hand trembled as she poured tea. As she spoke, Andrew and Roderick exchanged a telling glance.

It seemed evident to Andrew that the new girl must have had some role in this plot to hurt Justine. Her nervousness before the attack, and her disappearance immediately afterward were highly suspicious.

Mrs. Conroy chimed in, telling them how she had recently hired Celia.

"Could she have been the person you heard crying?" Andrew asked Justine.

Justine looked around at them all, wincing again as her head moved. "I don't know."

"We will check on her at once," Roderick said. "In the meantime, I believe you need to rest, daughter." He laid a gentle hand on Justine's shoulder, and looked at his wife.

"I will stay with Justine," Mary said, "and make sure she gets some rest."

"Mrs. Conroy, send another maid to help Mrs. Rawlings," Roderick ordered. "Someone who is exceptionally trustworthy."

"I'll send my daughter-in-law, sir," Mrs. Conroy said, nodding vigorously. "She is devoted to Justine."

"Fine." Roderick met Andrew's eyes, and Andrew knew he wanted to discuss this with him, without any of the ladies present. "Andrew, perhaps you will help Danvers and I question the servants?"

"Of course," Andrew replied. He gave Justine one more glance. She looked so pale, and the bruise was evident.

"I should like to help—" She tried to sit up.

"No!" Both Andrew and Roderick declared.

"You must rest, dear," Mary said gently.

"We will let you know what we learn," Roderick said, but Andrew doubted that Roderick was going to share all their fears with his daughter.

"You rest now," Andrew stated.

Something flickered in Justine's eyes. But he couldn't read her expression, and it was time to go help Roderick, anyway. "I'll check on you later," he told her, his tone soothing. Raising her fingers to his lips, he kissed them lightly. Her hand had warmed in the last few minutes. Perhaps she was feeling better.

As he left the room, preceded by Roderick, it occurred to Andrew that he rarely felt this worried.

Justine lay her aching head against the pillows Mrs. Conroy had brought in as Mrs. Conroy's daughter-in-law Pauline drew the drapes. Mary had settled down in a chair nearby and was sipping tea.

She closed her eyes, hoping to get some sleep. She didn't like the fact that her mother and Pauline were going to sit here and watch her rest, but it was evident they wanted to be sure she was well looked after. Besides, her head hurt too much to argue. The potion the doctor had given her had not taken effect yet.

With her eyes closed, she could ignore the soft whispers of sound coming from the two women, and pretend she was alone. Alone to think about Andrew.

Despite the horror of the attack, and the headache she now felt, she was aware of a strange feeling of hope.

Hope that Andrew was beginning to care.

His face has been most anxious when he peered at her. And his voice—he had sounded quite worried.

He cared . . . at least a little . . . she thought fuzzily.

"Ah, she is going to sleep already," Mary said, her voice barely audible.

Justine realized she must be smiling. No, she was not sleeping. She was merely going to rest, and dream of Andrew . . .

Andrew dropped wearily into a chair, and Edward pulled up one beside him.

"Can I get you anything, m'lord?" asked Jeeson.

"No, thank you," Andrew replied. The clock on the mantle said nearly eleven. He was ready for a good night's rest. If one could be found.

"Nothing for me either. Quite a day, eh?" Edward mused, as the butler bowed and left them in the small parlor adjacent to Andrew's study, where he liked to relax.

"That is true." Andrew ran a hand through his hair. "Quite a day." Between his and Roderick's questioning of the servants and speaking to the Bow Street runners, time had flown since the mysterious figure had struck Justine. Edward, good friend that he was, had offered to help. But none of them had been able to learn a thing that was helpful. No one but Justine and George had seen the dark-clothed figure. No one would admit to leaving the door unlocked. And no one had been able to locate Celia, the maid.

He had returned with Edward twice during that evening to check on Justine. The first time she had been sleeping in the library. The second time he learned she was awake, had been helped upstairs to her room, and was now resting there, guarded by her mother and a maid inside the room. The Rawlings had never been a family to have an overabundance of servants standing about, since they preferred privacy. But now several manservants stood in the corridors.

Roderick was taking precautions with his entire family. No one was to go anywhere alone.

Kevin had joined them, as well, but their last discussion with Roderick and one of the Bow Street runners had revealed nothing notable. Roderick had finally ordered everyone to get some rest.

On the way back to his townhome, Andrew had discussed with his friend the reasons for the attack on Justine. Edward concurred with his opinion that someone wanted to eliminate Justine because she was Andrew's fiancée.

"Do you have any idea who might want to do away with your fiancée?" Edward asked now, leaning forward.

"Yes." Andrew had been thinking about it all evening. One name leaped to mind. "I was told the maid, Celia, came recommended from someone in Lady Overbridge's household."

"Yes?"

"Lady Overbridge is a distant relative of Isobel Newmont. I believe Isobel could be behind this."

"Ahh haa," Edward said, nodding slowly. "Yes, that could be so. Isobel could be desperate to become a marchioness. Why, she was practically begging for your attention several weeks ago."

"Yes, and I wouldn't trust her brother for a moment," Andrew agreed. "He is entirely too greedy; I have heard he is in financial trouble. I intend to check on that tomorrow." He bent forward, and rubbed his head slowly.

"I would say you need a good night's sleep," Edward said. "And that you should be on guard, as well."

"I have taken extra precautions with my household already. Although I sincerely doubt that I need worry about my own well-being."

"No, you are probably not a target." Edward hesitated. "It is obvious you are most anxious about your fiancée."

"Well, of course. My poor Justine was injured; I shudder to think what might have happened if she hadn't seen her assailant before he hit her."

Edward studied him for a minute. "I don't believe I have ever seen you so concerned over a woman."

"Of course I am concerned! She is my fiancée, and I care—"

Andrew stopped.

A small smile was playing around Edward's mouth.

"I care for her well-being," Andrew finished, his tone more subdued. "She is a friend."

"Of course. It is just . . . you seem extremely concerned, Andrew."

Andrew looked down at his hands, which were tightly gripping the arms of his chair.

He *was* concerned. Very concerned.

More worried than he had ever been before about anyone in his life.

Chapter Eleven

Justine smoothed her skirt with unsteady hands as she sat in the blue parlor, waiting for Andrew to enter. The pale green fabric of her afternoon gown felt silky against her warm palms.

Her mother had lit extra candles because the day, which had started sunny, had grown increasingly dark. Now rain had begun to ping against the glass panes.

"I'll leave you two to talk," Mary said, smiling down at Justine fondly. "Shall I send in tea?"

"Yes, thank you."

It had been several days since the candlestick attack, and she was feeling considerably better. The headache was mostly gone now, although she tired easily. The physician visited her each day, and had told her the headaches would go away soon; and then she would feel like her normal self.

But she wondered if she could ever feel quite like her normal self again.

Because now she was quite convinced that someone was trying to harm her.

The incident with the arrow might have been attributed to a careless hunter. Or it could be seen as an attempt to injure any one of the young ladies at the garden party that day.

But the attack with the candlestick was a premeditated, deliberate attempt to injure her, or worse, kill her.

She shivered as the thought struck her for the hundredth time.

Who wanted to hurt her?

Judging from her father's and Andrew's concern, she believed they were certain, too, that she was a target.

She had to get better. She had to help find out who was responsible.

During the last few days she had seen Andrew only once, briefly. Charlotte and Kevin had been present, so they'd had no time alone together.

Andrew had looked fatigued himself, and had nothing new to report when questioned.

Justine had been hoping all day he'd stop in, and had insisted on coming downstairs earlier. When the butler had announced only moments before that Andrew was here, she had felt a rush of happiness that chased away any lingering aches.

Now she heard his firm footsteps against the marble floor of the hall, and then he appeared in the doorway.

"Good afternoon," Justine said cheerfully, proud that her voice sounded normal.

Andrew's face looked both weary and troubled. But as he walked to her, a smile lit his mouth.

"You look much better today," he said, and picking up her hands, bent forward to kiss her fingertips lightly.

Even that small gesture sent warmth flowing through Justine.

"I do feel much better," she said as he let her hands go. He pulled a chair closer to the sofa where she sat. "But you, Andrew, look fatigued," she continued, regarding him. "You must get some rest too. The Bow Street runners will locate my assailant, I am certain."

Andrew dropped into the chair, and ran his hand through his hair. "So far they have not, even with help from your father and uncle, Edward and myself, and Kevin."

Faintly, Justine heard music from the pianoforte, which Charlotte was playing in another room. Something more was bothering Andrew, she decided. He looked more uneasy than he had the other day.

"What else is wrong?" she asked, her tone sharper than she intended.

He sighed, not meeting her eyes.

"I know there is something."

He raised his eyes to meet her look. "Yes, there is something." For a moment he hesitated, and only Charlotte's music and the steady raindrops sounded in the parlor. Then he continued, frowning, "I am sorry to tell you this, but—I am afraid you will hear about it anyway."

"Yes?" Something tightened inside her. This appeared to be bad news.

"This morning the body of a young woman washed

up on the banks of the Thames. Bow Street believes it is Celia." He bent towards her, regarding her anxiously.

Justine gasped as an icy wave swept up her spine. "Are they sure?" Her voice was a croak.

"Not completely, but her description matches Celia's, and her clothes match the clothing she wore when you last saw her. They are calling upon relatives to identify her." His frown deepened, and Justine saw very real concern in his eyes.

"Oh, my word. The poor girl."

"The poor girl? She most certainly had a part in your injury!" Andrew exclaimed, his voice rising indignantly. He sprang up and began to pace. "Perhaps she felt sorry and couldn't live with the remorse after the attack on you, and she ended her life, but she deserved to feel guilty! You could have been killed, Justine."

"How do you know she took her own life?" Justine asked quietly. "Perhaps she was killed to keep her silent."

Andrew stopped abruptly. He gazed at Justine, and from the expression on his face she saw that he, too, believed this to be a distinct possibility.

"You could be right. I did not want to alarm you by suggesting this. I believe that it is possible that she was killed by whoever arranged the attack." His normally cheerful eyes bespoke of worry.

"That's why I said, the poor girl." Justine fought to keep her voice calm, but her heart was beating rapidly. Celia very likely had been murdered! She swallowed, studying Andrew again. She'd never seen him so agitated, and instinctively, she wished to try to calm him down. "Have you told my father?" She tried to sound serene.

"I sent a note to him earlier, but I understand he is with your uncle."

"Yes."

Andrew dropped into the chair again. Leaning forward, he said, his voice deadly serious, "This person or persons could try again to hurt you."

She couldn't help the shiver that ran through her. She was certain Andrew noticed it.

There was no reason to worry him more than he already was.

"They will not succeed," she said firmly. "I am well protected, as you can see. There are two footmen in the hall. My father should be returning any moment now."

A servant interrupted, with their tea and biscuits. After she left, Justine poured the tea with a hand that shook. She tried to breathe deeply of the aroma, hoping her heart would slow its anxious thumping. For a moment, only the sound of rain reverberated in the room. Charlotte had stopped playing the pianoforte.

"They may try again." Andrew considered his next words. "I am afraid, Justine—and Edward and your father agree with me—that you may be the target because you are marrying me."

"I had thought of that. There are many who might like to marry a marquis—or perhaps have a close relative married to a marquis."

"So this has occurred to you as well."

Justine nodded slowly. "It is the first thing I thought of."

"You are quite an intelligent young lady."

"Thank you." For a moment, Justine wished she

hadn't drawn that conclusion. It made her uneasy, to say the least.

They were silent, and Andrew's expression turned brooding. Justine waited, sensing he was giving thought to something more.

"They may try to hurt you again," he said after a few seconds. "I am most concerned, Justine."

"And I am grateful for your concern," she returned softly. Very grateful, she thought. His concern was indicative that he had strong emotions toward her! She felt as if a tiny glimmer of sunshine was brightening the gloom of the afternoon.

"Even with the best of protection, you could still be in danger. For your own safety, perhaps . . ." his voice dwindled.

"Yes?"

"Perhaps we should end our engagement now."

The words struck at Justine as hard as the blow from the candle. End their engagement?

It was a terribly distasteful thought.

Even though, a voice inside her asked, yours is a temporary engagement?

She desperately searched for words to indicate she didn't like the idea.

He looked at her. "You are still in pain," he observed.

"No, no, I am fine . . . but I do not believe that ending our engagement right now is the answer."

"You would be out of danger, at least temporarily."

"And so too you might be in danger," Justine pointed out. "The culprit could go after you." She smoothed her hands against the folds of her green gown.

"I doubt that. I believe the culprit was paid to get you out of the way so I might choose another fiancée."

"Then she, too, would be in danger." Justine's voice had grown raspy, and her heart felt heavy. "Unless, of course, you select the woman who this . . . culprit . . . wishes you to choose."

Andrew looked at her for a minute, then his mouth quirked up in a smile. "I doubt very much I would want to choose anyone who has sinister connections."

"Would you really know?"

"I believe I would."

"Oh." Justine could think of nothing to say to that. She leaned back on the sofa as relief crept through her. Her stiff hands relaxed.

"I would think," Justine began, her thoughts skipping forward rapidly, "that the best approach to this problem is to simply catch the culprit. Wouldn't that be better than crying off too early? Think of Charlotte and Kevin."

"Catching him is easier said than done," Andrew said, his expression solemn. His blue eyes studied her. "Although I am sure you are right, and that is indeed the best solution."

"Then that is what we must accomplish," Justine said briskly, hoping she sounded calm and practical. And that he couldn't hear her thudding heart.

Andrew sighed. "Yes." He straightened suddenly, sending her a warning look. "*We?* This is something that will be accomplished by myself, your father and our friends, along with the Bow Street runners. Not by you, Justine." His voice was stern.

Justine felt a momentary impatience. "I am perfectly capable of helping—"

"Not against a murderer!" Andrew declared, his whole face growing grim. "They attempted to hurt, perhaps murder you, Justine! And it's very likely, as you suggested, that they did kill Celia." His eyes began to blaze. "Do not even consider for a moment the foolish notion of helping us. No, you are to stay here and get well."

Andrew sprang up again, and this time he came over to the couch, leaning close to Justine. Taking her chin in his hand, he tilted it up and bent closer, so their faces were but inches apart.

Justine caught her breath as her heart leaped like a frog crossing a pond.

For a moment they stared at each other. Time seemed to stand still as the moment stretched. Justine was conscious only of Andrew's hand, warm and steady, cupping her chin. She felt his breath softly caress her face.

"I do not want you involved in anything to do with this sinister business," he said, his voice brooking no argument. "You are to stay here and get well. I will see to catching the culprit or culprits."

Justine could hear her heart thumping as she gazed into Andrew's eyes, locked on hers.

"I understand," she said faintly, swallowing. Justine had to fight the sudden desire to fling her arms around him.

"Good." He dropped his hand and moved back.

If only he would kiss her like he had a few weeks

previously! She could barely believe her strong desire to be held in his arms.

"I do not want you in any danger for my sake!" she said, her voice hoarse.

Andrew laughed. "Believe me, I will not court danger. But I am capable of taking care of myself."

"And I am not?" The words escaped before she could think.

"To be blunt, you know nothing of the devious workings of some people's minds."

"I have met many kinds of people; and I am well read; I do know how people's minds work," Justine protested, her heart still beating rapidly.

Andrew shook his head. "You can depend on myself and your father. We will do everything in our power to catch this culprit. You are to do nothing but get well."

She could not help but appreciate the fact that Andrew was concerned for her welfare and wanted her to recuperate. But she also did not like the fact that he wanted her kept out of any plans to catch the villain or villains.

"I will do my best." Justine had no desire to argue with Andrew. She did not add that she would promise nothing regarding her involvement in tracking down the assailant.

"In the meantime, we can end our betrothal, if we deem it necessary." He had gone back to his original idea. "Let us see what develops in the next few days."

Justine's heart sagged again.

Andrew pulled out his pocket watch. "I will bid you good-bye now; I am meeting Edward within the hour, and later I will speak to your father. I intend to begin working on a scheme to trap this villain. In two days, I must visit my estates up north; but by the time I return, I hope to have some plan in mind for catching this dastardly person."

He took Justine's hand and swiftly planted a kiss on her fingers. Before the warmth of his touch could spread completely through her, he bowed and left the room.

Justine sighed deeply after Andrew's footsteps receded down the hall. Closing her eyes, she conjured up his image as he'd leaned close to her.

The realization engulfed her, like a great gust of wind overtaking her and blowing her away.

She loved Andrew. She loved him!

Chapter Twelve

Part of Justine was ecstatic. To be in love with such a caring, wonderful, handsome man was thrilling.

The other part of her was tied up in knots of anxiety. She was uncertain as to his feelings. While he was always congenial, and appeared to care for her well-being, those could be the emotions of a good friend, not love.

What did he feel, she wondered, when he held her close? When he was near to her, their faces only inches apart. She wanted him to kiss her. Wanted it badly. Her heart beat rapidly and all she could think of was her desire to be held in his arms.

And he had seemed to enjoy kissing her too.

But what about their "engagement?" Was she going to be his pretend fiancée for only a matter of days?

She knew with sudden clarity that if he ended their engagement, it would break her heart.

Was there any chance that Andrew could grow to love her?

Justine mulled over the thought. The only way to discover the truth, she decided, was to find a way to catch the culprit behind these attacks.

And then to see what Andrew's feelings truly were.

Perhaps, she thought hopefully, he would decide to marry her because she was a suitable wife, and it would be an estimable match. They dealt tolerably well together.

But did she really want to enter into a match based on suitability, as some of her friends had done? As members of the ton often did?

No, that would never be enough for her! She loved Andrew, and wanted his love in return.

She must come up with a plan. A better plan than his. A plan of her own, that she could pursue by herself.

But what?

And *who?*

Who? she asked herself again.

Isobel's face came immediately to mind. Justine remembered the look on Isobel's face at the Seyling ball. Isobel was selfish and scheming. She was a woman who Justine could easily envision planning a rival's demise.

Justine thought briefly of Lady Agatha. That young woman was jealous, too, but not clever enough to launch a complicated plot to eliminate a rival. Besides, Agatha had been sent to an aunt's far away.

Justine recalled a whispered conversation between her father and mother when she was lying on the sofa the day after the assault. Father had said that Celia came recommended by the housekeeper from Lady Overbridge's household. Lady Overbridge was a distant relation of Isobel and Darren Newmont.

Could Isobel and her brother be the perpetrators behind the attacks?

It seemed all too plausible.

Justine spent much of the next two days in intense thought, considering what she could do to catch her assailant. The more she thought about it, the more she became convinced that Isobel was behind the schemes.

It was not only the whispered mention of Isobel's name during her father's conversation. The memory of Isobel's venomous looks at Count Seyling's ball remained firmly planted in her mind. After considering other possibilities, Justine was certain that Isobel and her brother were just the kind of nefarious people who were capable of plotting her demise. Hearing Isobel's and Darren's names bandied about by her parents served to reinforce her conviction.

Yes, Isobel was certainly capable of planning a murder. Selfish and grasping, money-hungry and nasty, the woman was likely to hatch a plan even without her brother Darren's help.

But she probably did have his help, Justine believed. Perhaps Darren had even been the man who struck her.

The thought of Darren, sneaking about in her home and hitting her with the candlestick, filled Justine with extreme loathing. She reached to pour herself some tea.

She must trap Isobel. And she must do it soon.

Because Isobel was probably even now plotting to eliminate her!

She might even have put the word out that she was looking for devious people to help her, people who could be bribed, as she had presumably bribed poor Celia . . .

Justine stopped, the teacup midway to her lips.

She could assume the identity of one of those people! Well, why not?

She placed her teacup back in its saucer with a clink.

If she pretended to be someone looking for work, any kind of work, someone who didn't mind being a party to murder, she could learn of Isobel's plans. She could even suggest a scheme, and trap Isobel into going along with it.

The more she thought about the idea, the more excited Justine became.

She tapped her fingers against the marble side table, the sound matching her increased heartbeat, as her thoughts sped along.

She could go to Isobel, pretending to be a lowly servant in the Rawlings household, someone with no scruples, who needed money. Isobel was so self-centered that Justine doubted she ever really looked at the faces of other women, especially those of the lower classes; so if she cloaked herself in servant's garb, Isobel would not likely recognize Justine. And she knew, from play-acting with her sisters when she was younger, that she could give a good imitation of a lower-class accent and speech patterns.

Her thoughts galloped away. Yes, she could act the part . . . but perhaps a disguise would be best, just in case she was wrong and Isobel did look at her face.

A mask. That was it. If she met her in the evening,

when it was growing dark, and she wore a mask . . . Justine jumped up and paced the room as she made her plans.

There were a number of masks in the Rawlings household. She and Charlotte had pulled them out of a trunk from the attic only a few weeks ago in order to decide on which ones to wear to the Viscount and Lady Tinton's masked ball next week.

A mask would disguise her perfectly.

Of course, she would need some help. It would be foolhardy to wander out alone, even masked, to approach Isobel and her brother. And she might need help slipping away from her well-guarded home.

Who could she trust?

Charlotte, or course.

Justine suspected that her sister would be hesitant to get involved in this scheme. She would worry and fuss.

But Charlotte owed her a huge favor. After all, it had been Justine's pretense at an engagement that had caused Father to agree to Charlotte's own betrothal. So Justine had no doubt she could persuade Charlotte to help her.

And Charlotte had a secret liking for drama as much as Justine. Justine thought back to her sister's announcement that she would elope to Gretna Green. Yes, Charlotte could act and keep a secret when necessary.

And perhaps, when Isobel was at last trapped and compromised, with her part in the schemes against Justine revealed, then Justine could find out what Andrew's feelings were.

Perhaps she would even be daring enough to suggest they make their betrothal a real one . . .

Justine sat for another hour, doing some long, hard thinking to perfect her plan.

"You what?" Charlotte gasped.

"I have a plan to trap Isobel. I have thought long and hard on it."

Justine had already expressed to her sister her conviction that Isobel and Darren were behind the attempts on her life. Now, perched on the lounge chair in Charlotte's room, she began to elaborate on her scheme.

"I will send round a note, asking to meet Isobel in the park in the evening, in the shadowy corner by the trees." Justine spoke firmly, seeing Charlotte's wary expression. "I will go, garbed as a servant, and wearing a mask. You, wearing a mask as well, will accompany me."

"Go unchaperoned?" Charlotte's eyes were wide. "Especially after what happened? And Father has us watched—"

"No need to worry, I've thought about that. We will have our maids accompany us with the footmen of their choice, and tell them we want to look like a gay party out for a stroll. We shall tell them it's a small prank. With the footmen along, I'm sure no one will protest, and the men should keep the young ladies occupied."

"But—"

"We will, of course, remain in the sight of the servants," Justine continued. "Our maids will not be surprised that we say we want to play a prank on Isobel; few like her, and servants gossip. I'm certain her reputation precedes her. And as far as Mother and

Father . . . we will tell them that we are going to rehearse with friends for a sketch we will present at Viscount Tinton's masquerade! That way they will not be suspicious."

Charlotte still looked dubious. "And then what?"

"I will tell Isobel I am a servant of Justine's, and I have heard she wants to eliminate Justine. For a fee, I will carry it out, and bring her proof afterwards that I have accomplished the deed."

"Proof? What proof?" Charlotte frowned at Justine.

"I'm not sure yet." Justine looked down at her fingers, which were twisting in her lap. She wished, suddenly, that Andrew was here. But she knew she couldn't confide any of this in him. He'd forbid her involvement. He would probably take steps to prevent her carrying out the plan.

She considered what she could bring as the supposed proof. Something that was known to belong to the Rawlings family.

She snapped her fingers triumphantly as a thought occurred to her. "My seed pearl brooch! Many people know that in Mother's family, Grandmama gave her three daughters jeweled brooches when they reached the age of sixteen; and Mama and her sisters have continued the tradition. I will indicate that I will bring the pin as proof. That should satisfy Isobel. And I will name a high price, so that Isobel thinks I am an accomplished villainess, and the plan is for real."

"How will you supposedly kill yourself?" Charlotte's voice was strained.

"I have thought of that too." Justine smoothed out her golden skirt. "Poison. I know enough from my reading to convince Isobel I have a harvest of night-shade with which to doctor Justine's bedtime drink."

Justine sat back, a smile tugging at her mouth. She couldn't help the satisfied feeling she had. It was an ingenious plan! She was sure it would work. She was certain that she was more intelligent than Isobel, and was positive she could act like a maidservant and pull it off.

Yet, she could feel her smile trembling ever so slightly. Nothing will go wrong, she assured herself staunchly.

Charlotte was silent, frowning. "I do not trust Isobel," she said after a few moments.

"I don't either. That is why, after this plan is set up, I am going to send a note to Edward and ask his help. He is Andrew's truest friend, and I am sure he will accompany us when we go to see Isobel for the second time with the proof that Justine is dead. Because other-wise, Isobel or Darren might try to kill me, as they did Celia."

"It is dangerous," Charlotte said, shivering. "Perhaps mad! There must be some other way to stop Isobel."

"I have no other choice." Justine leaned forward, intently regarding her sister. "Please, Charlotte. I pre-tended to be engaged when you needed me to; whether you think so or not, I did it to help *you*. Now I need you to help me succeed." When Charlotte still looked doubtful, Justine finished. "I need to do this, you see. Afterwards, I must determine if Andrew truly cares for me."

"What do you mean?" Charlotte furrowed her brow.

"The only plan Andrew has come up with is for me

to cry off from our betrothal. He feels that if we do this soon, then I will no longer be in danger." Justine got up and began to move restlessly about the room. She paused by the small clock on the mantle, listening to the low sound of its ticking as she stared at the Roman numerals on its face.

"I told him, that 'tis better to catch the culprit; and though he agreed, he did not come up with an alternate plan before leaving for his estates up north." She whirled abruptly, staring straight at Charlotte. "If he returns and we haven't found the proof we need that Isobel is behind this plot—and as I said I am certain she is—"

Charlotte nodded. "Kevin believes that too."

"Well, if we don't have proof, he will insist that I cry off." She found her hands clutching her skirt, wrinkling the smooth silk material. "Please, Charlotte. You were correct: I have fallen in love with Andrew. I want to find out if there is any chance that we . . . that we could have a future together. Please don't deny me the help I gave to you," Justine pleaded softly. Tears filled her eyes.

Charlotte let out a long breath. "Very well, Justine. But . . . I must insist we let Kevin in on the plan."

Justine had anticipated Charlotte's request, and already knew her answer. "Fine. But no one else."

Charlotte ran over to Justine and grabbed her hands.

"I knew you loved him," she said simply. "And I understand exactly how you feel. I just wish this plan was not so dangerous."

"There is no danger," Justine said, shaking her head. She hugged her sister tightly. "Thank you."

But inside, she was not as sure as she pretended to be.

*   *   *

Justine led the way through the park, her steps purposeful but unhurried. Charlotte walked by her side. The four servants chattered gaily, and Justine tried to act the same, relating amusing stories to Charlotte. The sweet smell of grass filled her nose, and the cheerful tones of the servants, plus the occasional neigh of a horse and other distant voices were soothing, normal accompaniments as they strode along.

The note she had sent round just yesterday to Isobel had been answered immediately—so fast, in fact, that Justine considered it further evidence that Isobel was behind the candle and arrow incidents. She had requested a meeting, claiming she could help Isobel eliminate her competition in the marriage mart, and naming the time and place she wished to meet. Isobel's response had been sent back with the very same boy who had brought the invitation.

Isobel scrawled, *Yes. I will meet you.*

Justine had spent the better part of the morning play-acting with Ginette and Arabella, who were glad to have their older sister join them in their games. It had not been difficult to convince her youngest sisters to let her act the part of a maidservant while they pretended to be princesses.

She had chosen the largest of the masks in the trunk, and now it lay rather uncomfortably against her face. But it hid her features completely.

Their entire party was masked, too, and appeared to be simply a jolly group heading out for an evening masquerade.

The air was cooler tonight than it had been for several days, and Justine had donned an old, no longer stylish cloak she'd found in the attic, the kind a lady might give to her maidservant when she tired of it. The gray folds hid her body and in fact, made her look plumper than her normal self. She was well disguised.

Justine quickened her step as they neared the trees in the corner. She observed that there were already two figures standing in the shadows . . . Isobel, and probably Darren, she guessed.

I'm a servant, Justine repeated to herself. She took a deep breath, the scent of flowers and warm green grass filling her as she moved forward. *I'm an experienced woman of the world who's accustomed to underhanded dealings.* She had repeated those words to herself for several hours, so that she could live the part she was playing.

As she drew near, she saw that Isobel was indeed with Darren. Justine waved her hand when they got closer, and, as they had been instructed, the servants stayed put. Only Charlotte followed Justine.

When Justine was a few yards away, Charlotte stopped too.

Now it was up to her.

Justine made her steps firm and confident.

"M'lady?" she said, her accent that of an uneducated London servant, her voice both respectful but assured, as one who had spent much time dealing with the aristocracy.

"Yes." Isobel's face betrayed an unappealing eagerness. "You said you had a plan to eliminate my competition?"

"Who are you?" Darren snapped.

Justine answered Darren first. "A servant in the

Rawlings household. That's all you need to know, governor. I've no intention of giving out a name." She made her voice haughty, despite the lower-class accent, and a lower pitch than usual.

Before Darren could say another word, she focused on Isobel. "I've heard tell that you seek to rid the marquis of his future bride, Justine Rawlings."

"Yes." Again, Isobel sounder eager.

Justine smirked, knowing it would show in her voice and posture. "I can help you."

"How do you know this?" Darren demanded.

Isobel sent her brother a quelling look. "Be quiet, Darren. I can handle this."

"I told you I'd handle things—"

"Look how far that has gotten us. You've botched every attempt so far." Isobel's scorn was evident in her voice, in her expression.

Darren began another protest, and Isobel snapped, "Be still. Let us hear what this woman has to say."

Justine bowed her head, as if used to doing so. "I have my ways of learning these things. For a price, I can see that Miss Rawlings is removed . . . permanently."

"Yes? How?"

Justine looked up again and had to suppress an overwhelming desire to smack the eager look away from Isobel's face. She tried not to focus on the fact that this woman very much wanted her dead.

"Poison," she said slowly, emphatically.

"Poison! Yes! That should work," Isobel said. "How will you poison her?"

"She takes milk and biscuits every evening before she retires." Justine drawled out the words for dramatic effect. "I usually am the one to bring them to her. 'Twill be easy enough for me to slip some poison in 'er milk." She had given much thought to the way she would dispose of herself; the lie came easily to her lips. "That should take care of 'er. Once you get rid of 'er, you can go on to become the next marchioness," she said craftily.

Isobel made no move to hide her gleeful expression. "Yes . . . but won't she know the poison is there?"

"I grow me own nightshade," Justine said proudly. "It makes a powerful mix; my own dear mother taught me just how much can be mixed in a drink without being detected, but enough to be lethal." She saw a dubious expression on Darren's face. "Got rid of me treacherous suitor quick enough when I caught him with me cousin." Her tone dropped, turning as dark as her menacing words.

Darren asked, "How will we know you've accomplished your task? We'll need proof that she is indeed dead."

"Aye, I'll bring ya proof."

"What kind?" Isobel asked.

Justine pretended to consider it for several seconds, as if the thought had not occurred to her previously. "Justine often wears a pearl brooch. Her mother gave it to 'er for a birthday; it's a fam'ly tradition. I will bring it to you."

"I've seen it," Isobel mused, although Justine doubted the woman noticed much about other people. Although, perhaps she did remember their expensive jewelry.

"Now, about the payment," Justine continued.

"Yes?" Isobel asked.

"I'll show you the brooch that night when you give me the money."

"How much?" Isobel asked.

Hoping the amount she was to name would sound on the high side but not ridiculous, Justine stated, "One hundred pounds." This was the amount she had decided on.

Darren gasped, and at first Justine's heart lurched. Was it too much?

Isobel pursed her lips.

"I want to live the good life," Justine said. "No more serving other people. This will be enough for me to disappear afterwards. You'll not have to worry about seeing me ever again. I'm going to the Americas."

"It is high . . . but justified, given the fact she will really be gone . . . Are you sure you can do the job?" Her voice sharpened, as she looked down her nose.

"Yes," Justine replied resolutely. "I am positive." She held her head high, as if she was challenging Isobel to think otherwise. She placed her hands on her hips, staring through the eyeholes in the mask.

Apparently, her confidence impressed Isobel that she was capable of the task.

"Fine," Isobel said, "but I must have that proof before I hand over the money."

"Certainly. And"—Justine added the thought she'd had late in the day—"I will need some kind of advance, something to assure me that you do indeed want me to complete this job." She made herself sound cunning, as if she'd done this kind of thing before.

Darren glanced at Isobel, who shrugged.

"Your brooch will do," Justine said, moving her hand in a grasping gesture towards the ruby pin on Isobel's dress.

"This? I'm not giving you this," Isobel protested.

"Then money."

"Darren, give her five pounds." Isobel named the amount carelessly. "Will that do?"

"Until we meet again," Justine said, glad the mask hid her triumphant feelings. Isobel had fallen for the plan! "I will send another note 'round tomorrow as to what day I will do the deed."

Justine stood still as Darren shuffled forward, glowering beneath Isobel's bossy gaze. He handed her the money, his eyes resentful.

Justine grasped it eagerly, dipped her head, then, with a swirl of her cape, turned and strode off. Charlotte followed her meekly, as they had agreed on, back to the others.

She'd done it! She'd done it! Justine was certain her performance of a greedy serving maid was the performance of her life.

Justine purposefully did not look back until they joined the servants. A quick glance then showed her that Isobel and Darren still stood in the shadowy corner, apparently having a heated discussion. She could hear Darren's voice, though not the words.

Darren was probably not happy with Isobel's decision to get someone else involved in eliminating Justine, she guessed. But Isobel had gotten her way.

Justine tried to hide her feelings of triumph as she

departed with Charlotte and the servants, walking to a pathway, talking and laughing like any party of young people.

She tricked Isobel!

Now the rest of her plan should be far easier.

She allowed herself a smile.

Chapter Thirteen

Justine sat in the green parlor, trying to work on her embroidery as she waited. It had grown warmer today, and between the warm, humid air and thoughts of her scheme to reveal Isobel as a potential murderess, she was having trouble concentrating. Her embroidery was not creating its usual soothing affect.

She had sent a note round to Edward earlier in the day, asking him to call this afternoon on a matter regarding Andrew. Since Andrew had told her father he would ask Edward to check up on her well-being, she had no doubt he would call.

Then she had spent the morning playacting again with Ginette and Arabella. Her sisters had been delighted to play the parts of ladies of quality while she played the role of a subservient but cunning maid.

Although Justine had felt uneasy prior to yesterday's meeting with Isobel, she was feeling more confident now. She knew Edward would be astounded by her plan, and probably worried. She hoped he would not be overly so; and she wished she felt no unease at all.

She sighed, finding her hands damp once again. She wiped them on the old cloth she kept handy, and then thrust her embroidery back into the carpetbag. She was in no mood to do more work.

Now that she had fooled Isobel into thinking she was a servant intent on killing Justine, the rest of the scheme should be easier, she reminded herself. She would reassure Edward of that fact.

And when Andrew returned, they could greet him with the news that Isobel had been trapped, and in front of several people had paid to have Justine killed.

And then she would see what he wanted to do about their pretend engagement.

Would he still want to cry off? Would he extend their engagement further?

And what were his true feelings regarding *her*?

The assured steps of their butler against the marble floor alerted Justine that there might be a visitor. The door to the parlor was open, a slight breeze between the door and windows stirring the air, and Danvers rapped lightly on the edge of the door.

"Yes?" she asked, trying to sound tranquil

"Miss Justine, Mr. Edward Collingsforth is asking to see you. Are you at home?"

"Send him in. And please have one of the maids bring us tea and biscuits."

She smoothed her hands over her skirt as she heard Danver's footsteps recede. Faintly, she could hear the laughter of her younger sisters somewhere outside in the garden, and then her brothers' voices. Walter and George were playing with the younger Rawlings girls.

They were fortunate, Justine mused, to be young and carefree . . . without adult burdens. For a moment, those burdens weighed heavily on her, and her shoulders sagged.

Danvers' footsteps were returning, with another pair echoing beside his. Justine straightened her spine, and forced a smile as Edward entered the room.

"How nice to see you," she murmured.

"Miss Justine." Edward took the hand she extended and bowed formally over it.

"You are well, I hope?" she asked as he seated himself in a side chair.

"Yes, and yourself?"

"Fine. Have you heard from Andrew?" It bothered Justine that she had not.

"Only one short message, to ask that I let him know if anything is amiss."

"Nothing is amiss," Justine said, but her pulse rate had become more rapid.

They spoke for several minutes about the weather, the upcoming masked ball at the home of Viscount Tinton, and Justine's younger siblings. Edward and Lawrence had a younger brother at Eton who apparently was a good friend of Walter's, and Edward described one of their escapades.

A maid who had been with the family since Justine was a young girl entered, smiling and bearing a tray with tea and freshly made scones.

"Right from the oven, dearie," she said.

"How wonderful! You must try these; they are cook's masterpiece," Justine said, offering the platter to Edward.

"Indeed I shall." He helped himself, and Justine poured tea.

"Anything else, Miss Justine?" the maid inquired.

"Thank you, Elsie, this is fine." Justine smiled at her, and the young woman left.

She stirred sugar into her own tea, and milk.

"Delicious," Edward said, savoring the scone.

He appeared to be relaxed. Now was a good time to reveal her plan.

"Speaking of escapades," Justine began, keeping her voice light. "I have one to tell you of. A plan I myself hatched, actually, and with which I could use your help."

"Yes?" Edward's cheerful expression told Justine he thought it was some silly girl's prank.

"Like Andrew, and you, and my father, I am convinced that Isobel—and her brother—are behind these attacks on me." She paused, watching Edward's face.

His smile had disappeared. In its place was a serious expression.

"Yes?" he said cautiously.

"And, as I told Andrew, we must catch the culprit."

Edward hesitated, then nodded. Apparently he was unsure of just how much he should say to Justine.

"I know my father and Andrew would like to shelter me from this problem, but it can't wait." Her voice took on a more acerbic note than she'd planned. "I want to resolve things before Andrew returns."

Edward started to protest. "There is no need—"

Justine held out her hand. "Please, hear me out."

Edward stopped, and she continued.

"I spent several days devising a plan, and brought Charlotte in on it. I sent a note to Isobel, asking for a meeting, and claiming I could help her eliminate her competition."

Edward's eyes grew wide. "You what?"

Justine went on. "I disguised myself as a masked serving girl, and went, along with Charlotte and four other servants, to meet Isobel in the park yesterday evening." Seeing the concern spread over Edward's face, she rushed on. "Please don't worry. Charlotte and I were well chaperoned by four people, and we all wore masks, disguised as a party of revelers who were to rehearse a scene."

"But, Justine—"

"I proposed to eliminate myself." Justine went on calmly. "I acted the part of a greedy servant perfectly; I proposed to poison Justine Rawlings for a high price, and Isobel believed me."

"She did?"

"Yes, and her brother did too, although he was somewhat reluctant to go along with the plan. I told Isobel I had knowledge of the poisonous powers of the nightshade plant; I have read about it, Edward, and I am quite aware of its deadly potential. I sent a note today, promising to meet Isobel two evenings from now, the night before Viscount Tinton's masked ball, with the proof of Justine's death—my seed pearl brooch. She believed me and agreed to the plan. I even asked for an advance on the money, and she gave it to me." Justine sat back, watching mixed emotions chase each other on Edward's face.

Edward opened his mouth, but for a moment not one word came out.

He coughed, and began again. "Justine, you have *no* idea how dangerous—"

"It was not dangerous. I was well chaperoned."

"Even so—Isobel and her brother are scheming liars, and cannot be trusted." Edward's face had grown darker.

"That's why I need your help with the rest of my plan. But you have to admit, it is a good plan; we shall catch Isobel in the act of paying for my demise, and with witnesses, that should be all the proof we need." Her heart beat rapidly as she said the words.

"I admit, it was a clever plot; but it is entirely too dangerous for you to be involved any further. I shudder to think what Andrew would say if he finds out."

"He will find out," Justine responded calmly. "But afterwards, when it is over. He is not due back yet."

"I can send him a note now," Edward warned, "telling him. I feel responsible for your well-being, Justine."

Justine had suspected Edward would react this very way. "You can send a note, but he is still at his estate in the north country; it will take several days for the note to get there, and several days for him to return." She couldn't quite hide the triumph from her voice. She had thought of everything, and planned for her meeting with Isobel to be well over by the time Andrew returned.

Edward stared at her.

There was silence for a minute. Then he coughed

again. "You have thought of everything, have you not?" he asked, his voice rasping.

"I believe so." Seeing Edward's concern, Justine softened her tone. "I must do this. I have to find out— I have to have proof that Isobel is the one behind these attacks, and have this taken care of before Andrew returns."

"Why?"

"Because—" She looked down at her hands. She hadn't realized she was twisting her fingers until that moment. "Because . . . I want to find out what Andrew plans to do . . ."—she looked back up at Andrew's closest friend—"about our betrothal."

"What do you mean?"

"I mean—he has indicated he might want me to cry off early, to protect myself." Justine swallowed. Andrew had confided that he'd told Edward the truth of their false engagement. "If I no longer need protection, he will have to decide if we should continue this charade so that Charlotte and Kevin may marry. I–I do not wish to hold him to an engagement he does not want; but I also want to find out if there is any . . . any chance . . ." Her voice faltered, and sudden tears filled her eyes. She looked away.

Edward was silent, and when he spoke, his voice was gentle. "You care about him a great deal, don't you?"

She looked back at him, and nodded. "But . . . please don't tell him. I need to find out if he . . . if he cares for me too."

"I believe he does," Edward said, his expression full of empathy.

But Justine shook her head. "Cares for me as a family friend, perhaps. As for anything else . . . after Isobel is compromised, I will know better. Please do not interfere."

"I can't let you run into danger." Edward reverted back to the first topic, and Justine felt relief. No one but Charlotte knew her true feelings for Andrew; except, now, Edward suspected. Still, she had not admitted the truth, that she was in love with Andrew.

"There will be no danger . . . and you can be assured of that, since I hope you and possibly a Bow Street runner, or one of your servants, will accompany me. You will be the witness I need to prove that Isobel is guilty."

Edward nodded. "It is a clever plan; but we must make some changes. I will get someone to disguise themselves as you—"

"No! She has seen me and heard my voice; only I can play the part." Seeing the consternation on Edward's face, she went on. "I will be in no danger, Edward; you, your servant, and Charlotte and Kevin will be present. Isobel will not dare to try anything once I have proven her guilt. In fact, when I do reveal myself, I was thinking we should ask her to leave the country—"

"A fine idea," Edward agreed, his voice taking on a sarcastic note, "except for one thing."

"What is that?"

He leaned forward. "Isobel and Darren in all likelihood had Celia killed. They probably intend the same fate for you, the servant."

"I am aware of that. I discussed it with Charlotte. But

Isobel will be revealed as a murderess long before they could put that plan into action."

"I consider it too risky. I am not in favor of this plan."

"It is already working. With or without you, I will be meeting Isobel and pretending that I have killed Justine. If you are not there, I will be disappointed, but I will be safe. Kevin and Charlotte will accompany me. I did wish," she finished, her tone wistful, "that you could be there to report all that happened to Andrew. I am positive your telling would hold the utmost weight."

Edward's mouth had turned downwards into a frown. "I did not say I wouldn't be there. I merely said I was not in favor of this scheme. Now then, seeing you are adamant, why don't you give me the details of the time and place."

Justine spent the next few minutes telling Edward the details of her plan. "This way, you can get there well before we do at nine o'clock, and hide in the bushes. I have written a note telling Isobel that I have given Justine a pinch of nightshade already to make sure she feels unwell and retires early. I will see the note is delivered on the proper day."

"I will be present. I will come forward only after Isobel has paid you the money for the supposed murder; then we will tell her she is compromised, and order her to leave the country. I will bring a servant with me or a Bow Street runner."

"Good." Now that she had Edward in reluctant agreement with her plan, Justine took a deep breath, feeling relief slowly seep through her limbs.

Her plan was proceeding as she had hoped. It would be completed in several days. All was well. It was almost as good as done, she told herself firmly.

But after Edward took his leave, still appearing worried about her scheme, she wondered if she was being overconfident.

No, she told herself, I'm merely being realistic. What could go wrong? She would be well supervised; Isobel would be caught; and then all would be well.

Perhaps Andrew would even discover that he had deep feelings for her.

She fantasized for several minutes about Andrew's return, imagining him holding and kissing her, and declaring his love.

If only things could be as rosy as she hoped!

She prayed things would go well, and that she would get the happy ending she so vividly pictured.

"That's it, Bradley," Andrew said, dismounting from his horse. "I believe that covers everything for this estate." A young groom ran up to see to his horse.

The manager of his familial estate not far from Dover, nodded as he, too, dismounted. "Very good, my lord. I shall immediately see to having repairs done on the roofs of the two cottages." Another groom, even younger, took the reins of the second horse.

"And you will let the Forrest family know we will be building a small cottage for their eldest son; it should be completed just before his marriage," Andrew said. "And then he will have to look no further for other work; we have need of him right here."

"Yes, my lord." The middle-aged estate manager

nodded. "I couldn't agree more. Though your uncle took care of the estate, and would have ordered the roof repairs, he was very cautious; he would have hesitated to build another cottage. I am glad to see you will put some money into the estate. It will help it to thrive."

"Cautious? Some would call it miserly," Andrew said with a laugh.

"Indeed." Bradley grinned.

"And as of this week, I am giving you a raise," Andrew continued, and named a fair rate. "According to my records, it was four years since Uncle Elias gave you one."

Bradley's face brightened considerably. "Thank you, my lord!"

"I shall expect weekly reports, as my uncle did."

"Of course," the older man assured him.

As they left the stables, a footman appeared. "My lord, there is an urgent message for you, come just now from London."

Urgent? Andrew hastened his step.

It could only be from Edward. Only he knew Andrew was here.

Andrew's visit to his estates up north had been only partly necessary. While he was anxious to see to things on his estates, he was also anxious to put into motion the plan he had been devising to try to catch the person or persons responsible for causing harm to Justine.

He had let it be known he was traveling north; he had made the journey, but spent only a single day at his estates there, cramming in the visit as quickly as he could, and leaving instructions to be carried out until he could get there again. Then, he had secretly, with a minimum of servants, doubled back. He had stopped to check on this particular estate because it was only a day away from London, and he had visited here only briefly in the last month. But tomorrow he planned to leave late in the day, to secretly return to London after dark. With his whereabouts presumed to be up north, he hoped to disguise himself and see what he could find out about Isobel and Darren.

No one, except for Edward, knew his itinerary for the journey. He had told his best friend so that, if there was an emergency, he could be reached.

Was there such an emergency now?

A liveried servant waited with a sealed note, and he took it, hurrying into his study.

"Thank you." Andrew dismissed the servant, then tore the note open.

It was indeed from Edward. He quickly scanned the contents.

Justine had hatched a plot to trap Isobel and Darren—she had disguised herself as a servant, willing to poison Justine Rawlings for a fee—she was going to bring proof of Justine's "death" to Isobel—Edward, a servant, or a Bow Street runner would be present, hidden in the bushes when Isobel paid her—he thought Andrew should know—

As he rapidly read Edward's words, Andrew felt his heart turn into a block of ice.

Justine could be in grave peril. She had no idea how dangerous people like Isobel and Darren could be.

They might even have recognized her, and were setting a trap themselves.

His very blood was frozen.

Justine. Justine. What if something happened to her? His whole being was filled to the brim with fear for her.

Edward's urgings for him to consider coming home early were unnecessary. Already he was moving towards the study door.

"Smith!" he called to the butler. "I've an urgent summons from London. I must prepare to leave at once."

Smith was there in seconds. "Yes sir. Very good, my lord."

Andrew ran up the stairs to gather his things. There was no time to waste.

He must get to Justine.

A near-panic feeling bubbled inside Andrew as he reached the top of the steps. It was a feeling that was totally foreign to him.

He had never felt this extreme concern, this anxiety, for anyone, ever before. He practically ran down the upstairs hall.

It was precisely at the moment when he entered his bedroom that Andrew knew exactly why he was so very concerned with Justine's welfare.

He had fallen in love with his supposed fiancée.

Chapter Fourteen

The hours were passing with excruciating slowness.

Justine found herself tugged between opposing feelings—both anticipating, and dreading, tonight's meeting with Isobel and Darren.

On one hand, she couldn't wait for the meeting. She would do what was necessary in order to trap Isobel, and then her mission would be accomplished. She would triumph. And when Andrew returned to London, it would be a fait accompli.

And then she could find out what his feelings were, and what he wanted to do regarding their pretend betrothal.

Yet she feared the meeting too . . . because what if her carefully planned scheme led her to finding out that Andrew held only feelings of friendly warmth towards her? She couldn't bear thinking about it. Neither did she want to consider the possibility of anything in her plan going awry.

She reassured herself that all would be well as she stared out of the window at the gray day that heralded rain. It was better to know the truth, even if it wasn't pleasant. Better to know now if Andrew had only friendly feelings.

But what if he did care for her? Maybe, with the threat of Isobel out of their way, he would discover he held more serious feelings toward her.

She wavered back and forth between hope and gloom during the afternoon hours.

And then there were moments of anxiety. What if all did not go well with their meeting? What if Isobel didn't show up?

No, everything would be fine. She tilted her chin up. She *must* think positively.

Charlotte, too, was unsettled, Justine observed. Justine knew her sister was unnerved about tonight's meeting, and frankly worried. Charlotte paced during the afternoon, only scuttling upstairs when their father came in, not wanting to appear openly nervous.

"I wish we were not going," she whispered to Justine. "I wish I had never agreed to this plan. It is too risky."

"There is no risk," Justine soothed, deliberately making her voice confident. "Between Kevin, Edward, and his men, we will be quite safe."

Charlotte sent her a look. "Do you not wish that Andrew was here?"

"Yes," Justine admitted. "But if he was, I probably would have changed the plan. I must carry this out by myself."

"Still, I don't feel comfortable."

"Kevin will be with us," Justine pointed out. He had agreed without too much protest, because, Justine was sure, he was afraid they might go with or without him. And he was protective of Charlotte. "And it will be done quickly."

The late afternoon hours dragged on. The clock's ticking, seeming louder than usual, echoed through the library. Justine found herself unable to concentrate on her favorite Shakespeare volumes, nor on any of the romantic novels she so enjoyed; and finally gave up.

She wondered if Edward had sent a note to Andrew regarding her plan. But even if he had, Andrew could not possibly return in time to stop it. He was up north, more than two days away.

When he came home it would be done, and Isobel, she hoped, would be out of the country—or perhaps even in prison.

They ate a light supper. Mary and Roderick had long had plans with one of Mary's brothers and his wife to attend the opera, and they departed shortly after the meal.

With the younger children upstairs involved in their own games before bedtime, Justine and Charlotte announced they were going to turn in early, and went to their rooms to prepare for the meeting.

The day had grown steadily cooler, with a persistent wind and the promise of rain. A good day, Justine told herself, a truly fitting day for a secret plot!

She changed swiftly, then pulled back her long, dark hair so it would be hidden within the cloak's folds. Garbed in the clothes of a maidservant to nobility, she reached for the elaborate mask that would hide her face. She studied the silver-colored mask for a moment, then picked up the hooded cloak and the reticule that contained her pearl brooch.

She stepped down the hall to Charlotte's room, glad that Father no longer had so many servants posted about the halls. Since the last week had been so quiet, he had relaxed, except when they went out. Rapping softly, she heard Charlotte's "Come in."

Charlotte, too, was nearly ready. Justine thought her face looked quite pale.

"We will be fine," Justine told her sister firmly, giving her a brief smile.

"I hope so," Charlotte whispered.

Justine moved forward, and handed Charlotte her own dark blue mask. "Let us go."

Charlotte picked up her cape and silently followed Justine down the backstairs.

They stopped at the bottom of the stairs, and Justine looked both ways, ascertaining that this wing was quiet. They proceeded to slip out the side door near the rose garden, where tall bushes hid them instantly. Once outside, they donned their masks and cloaks. Justine sniffed the romantic, reassuring scent of roses before she led the way through the gardens to the outer most bushes.

Kevin, garbed as a footman, was already waiting.

"Are you ready?" Justine asked.

He nodded. "Yes." He donned his own mask.

He led the way through London's streets to the park. On a nicer evening they would have passed many couples out for a stroll, as they did the previous time they'd been out. But this evening, with the wind blowing and clouds darkening the sky, there were few groups out and about. They passed one group of revelers who were singing boisterously, and Justine guessed the young people may have been imbibing overmuch. One young man, who she recognized as the younger son of an earl, was singing in a decidedly slurred voice.

Kevin led them firmly beyond the group, and onto a side path. Here they passed a couple embracing.

Soon this will be over, Justine told herself. And perhaps, someday, Andrew would embrace her that very same way—with a mixture of delight and desire.

The wish to see Andrew was almost overwhelming. It shook Justine to her toes, and she recognized how very much she loved him.

If only he was here now!

But that was impossible. She must do this herself, set her mind on the task at hand. She must assume the persona of a scheming servant, and keep her mind on the business at hand—murder. The "murder" of Justine Rawlings.

She walked confidently, her steps firm and her head high, as if arriving in triumph to the meeting.

When they reached the section of the park where she was to meet Isobel, she scanned the perimeter. There was no sign of anyone.

She prayed that Edward and his men were already there, well hidden. They should have been there for some time now.

And where was Isobel?

As she drew closer to the most shadowy corner, a figure stepped forward—Isobel.

Like Justine's party, Isobel was masked. But Justine recognized her dark blue gown and the haughty angle at which she held her head. Apparently, this time Isobel had come alone. Justine felt some surprise at that fact.

Justine moved forward until she stood close to Isobel. Kevin and Charlotte stopped a few yards behind.

"It is done." Justine's voice rang clear. She managed to sound immensely pleased with herself.

Isobel's hand fluttered. "Justine is dead? You have the proof?" Her mask could not hide the eagerness in her voice and posture as she bent forward.

"Yes." Justine pulled forth her reticule, and fished inside it. She held up her own pearl brooch. "I took this from her not an hour ago."

"Let me see." Isobel stepped closer.

"Let me see the money," Justine demanded, as if used to taking control of assignations such as this one.

Isobel hesitated, then nodded. "The money . . ." She pulled a purple satin pouch hanging from her arm.

Justine stood still, without speaking, and waited until Isobel opened the pouch. She removed silver and gold pieces. They clinked musically against each other, unnaturally loud in the quiet park.

"See?" Isobel held them up in her gloved hands.

"Very good. Now I wish to count the money, and then you will get the brooch."

As if she was having trouble parting with the amount, Isobel handed it over to Justine very slowly.

Justine made a gloating sound, and rapidly counted.

It had worked! Her plan had worked!

She recounted the coins, just to be sure, her heart beating quickly. It was all there!

Isobel had admitted paying to kill Justine! She had the money as proof!

For several seconds, Justine felt sheer, complete triumph.

"It is the correct amount," she declared loudly. That was her signal to Edward.

She heard a noise in the brush, and held her breath, expecting Edward to burst out beside them, ready to announce he had heard every word.

Then she heard another rustling sound, and from behind tall bushes, a cloaked figure approached. Darren.

The moon emerged from clouds to gleam on the pistol he thrust from beneath the folds of his cloak.

The gun was aimed directly at her.

Chapter Fifteen

Justine's heart skittered to a stop, and a horrid, cold feeling encased her entire body.

For a moment, all she could do was to stare at the gun in Darren's hand. Behind her, she heard Charlotte emit a strangled gasp.

"You didn't really expect to go free with that money?" Darren sneered, taking a step closer.

Justine kept her head held high, though she felt as if her legs were stuck to the ground. She had never seen a gun so close. "Indeed I did," she forced herself to say, her confident tone belying her rapid heartbeat.

A servant, also holding a gun, had appeared behind Darren. His gun was aimed behind Justine. She refused to turn away from Darren's eyes, but she suspected, hearing another gasp from her sister and a growl from Kevin's direction, that this one was aimed at Charlotte.

"You believe I would come unprepared for treachery?" Justine parried, her voice sarcastic. "You have much to learn."

Isobel started. "That voice—" She focused on Justine.

"Shut your mouth," Darren snapped, glancing at Isobel. "I'm taking over now."

Isobel started at his nasty tone. At the same time, more sounds came from the opposite side of the bushes from where Isobel and Darren were standing.

Seconds later, Edward and a manservant emerged, with their own guns cocked at Darren and Darren's servant.

"Good evening, Isobel," Edward said, his voice as pleasant as if he'd met her on an evening's stroll.

Isobel sucked in her breath audibly, taking a step back.

"Don't move," the manservant ordered. Or was he a Bow Street runner? Justine wondered.

"As you can see, I have plenty of witnesses that you plotted to murder Justine Rawlings," Justine declared, still in her lower-class accent.

"And we have heard every word," Edward added, a sarcastic smile on his face.

"You—" Isobel choked out.

Darren snickered suddenly. "Dudson!"

At his call, another manservant stepped into the clearing. His gun was aimed at Edward.

Justine's heart leaped into her throat. For a second, a desire to laugh warred with a desire to scream. There were so many players here, it was almost ridiculous.

Except that more of the weapons were aimed at her

and her friends than on her enemies. They were surrounded, outnumbered! Fear gripped her.

Darren and Isobel had anticipated her plans to have
people hidden in the bushes—and had done the same
exact thing themselves.

With all these people holding pistols trained on each
other, it would seem that she had only her wits to get
them out of this mess.

Her thoughts tumbled, stuck; and she ordered herself
to think clearly.

"Isobel," she began after a moment. "With all these
people present—all these witnesses to your admission
of murder—someone is bound to talk." She stared at the
haughty villainess. She strove to keep her voice normal,
proud even; and was pleased that she almost succeeded
in sounding like a scoundrel herself. "You shall be
revealed as a murderess, and branded by society. No
decent man—certainly not a marquis—shall ever marry
you. Your name will be whispered with contempt—"

"Stop that!" Darren interrupted.

"My servants are loyal," Isobel snapped at the same
time.

"Servants can be bribed," Justine said, hoping she
didn't sound desperate. She wanted to sound confident
and convincing. "With all these people disappearing,
questions will undoubtedly be asked. Fingers will start
pointing to you and your household." She noted that the
servant to the left of Darren was beginning to look
dubious. She pounced on that. "Yes, indeed, there will
be those who will offer money for their story—or worse
yet, demand money of *you,* Isobel, to keep you quiet—"

"Enough!" Isobel said. "I will listen to no more of this nonsense! Darren?"

From behind her, Justine heard Charlotte make a choking sound.

A sinking feeling was encompassing her. This is how a drowning man feels, she thought. What if she was outmaneuvered? All could be lost.

She would never see Andrew again. She would never be able to tell him how she felt.

She made a Herculean effort to sound strong. "If you think to kill me, think again. I shall return to haunt your every step."

This time Isobel recoiled.

"Yes, and I shall enjoy doing so," Justine said in her most menacing tones, pressing whatever slight advantage she might have.

"Don't listen to her!" Darren cried out. "Isobel! We shall kill her and the others, and be done with it."

"Don't be a fool. Use your head, for once," Edward declared, looking directly at Isobel. "Should your brother kill the young lady, and I kill him"—at this Darren visibly blanched—"and your manservant kills me, there will be too many bodies to dispose of and too much explaining to do. You will never be able to extricate yourself from this mess."

"I will manage," Isobel said tightly. But she cast her brother a look.

"Not easily." This from Kevin.

Did Justine imagine just a hint of uncertainty in Isobel's tone? Justine hazarded a guess that Darren's declaration of "taking over" was not sitting well with Isobel.

"How will you be able to manage?" Justine asked

sardonically. "I have taken the precaution of leaving a note behind, telling of your plans, in case I do not return home. My sister is awaiting me."

"I don't believe you," Isobel huffed. "Darren? Let's get on with it."

But Darren was looking hesitant now, as Edward's gun remained fixed on him.

Isobel, staring at Justine, took no notice of her brother.

"Any last words?" Isobel asked mockingly.

Darren's pistol pointed straight at her. It would be the first to be fired.

But she had one more card to play.

"Tell Andrew I love him," Justine said dramatically.

At Isobel's startled exclamation, Justine tore off her mask, then faced Darren defiantly. "You are not planning to kill a servant; you are attempting to murder a lady of quality," she said scathingly, as Darren's gun wavered in his suddenly unsteady hand. "This will not go unavenged! You both shall pay the highest price for your treachery, rotting in prison! Andrew shall seek you out, and avenge my death!"

"The devil he will!" Darren said.

"Speaking of the devil . . ." The smooth, masculine voice could only come from one person.

Andrew!

From the side closest to Isobel, Andrew emerged from the shadows, a pistol cocked and trained right at Isobel's head.

Excitement and wonder burst through Justine, followed by relief and confusion. Justine wanted to laugh and cry.

"At the first shot—from *anyone*—Isobel will die," he

said, and there could be no arguing with the determination in his voice, or his stance. "Now, Isobel, call off your people. *At once.* Unless you are prepared to meet your Maker in Justine's place."

Isobel began to shake. "N–n–no."

"I have no compunctions about shooting a murderess. Call them off—now!"

Isobel waved a trembling hand. "Darren, Dudson, Brown, put your guns away." The servants lowered their weapons, but Darren still held his.

Andrew shifted closer to Isobel, steely determination in the set of his jaw.

"Darren! I don't want to die!" Isobel cried. "Please!"

"Do you want to be responsible for your sister's death?" Justine asked, staring at Darren.

Slowly, Darren lowered his pistol.

"A wise choice." Andrew sounded completely unruffled. He kept his weapon trained on Isobel. "Now, Isobel, I shall remove the gun once your brother and men are disarmed."

Edward and his servant, whom Justine recognized now as a Bow Street runner who had visited their home after she was struck, rapidly proceeded to do just that. Kevin moved forward to help them disarm the three men as Andrew stood silently, his gun still threatening Isobel.

Justine stepped over to Isobel, and ripped off her mask.

Isobel's face was bright red, her expression mortified.

"This was . . . this was all Darren's fault!" she accused, and turned toward Andrew with a pleading expression.

"It wasn't!" Darren yelled.

"Yes, yes, 'tis true."

"No! That's a lie!" Darren looked like he wanted to strangle her. He made a convulsive movement as Edward pulled Darren's now empty hands behind his back. The Bow Street runner handed over a length of rope.

"No more lies, Isobel," Andrew declared. With all the men disarmed, he finally let his hand holding the pistol drop to his side.

And turned to regard Justine.

She recognized relief in his brief look.

And . . . something more. Something unreadable.

Overwhelming hope slammed into her as their looks locked and held. Her pulse beat as rapidly as it had before.

"We have many witnesses here," Andrew said to Isobel, whose complexion had gone from red to pasty white. "You now have two choices. Be prosecuted as a would-be murderess, with all the ensuing public outcry and scandal—or leave the country. For at least ten years."

Isobel gasped.

"We will file the papers with my solicitors," Andrew continued in a most pleasant voice, while Edward sent his friend a wide grin. "If ever, upon your return, you cause even the tiniest amount of trouble to Justine—or to anyone else—we will have the proof we need to ruin you."

"You can't mean that," Isobel said faintly. "Banish me from my own home?"

"Better than prison, I would think. But it is your choice." His voice was calm and cool.

"Yes, it's better," Darren practically spat out. "But not much!"

"No! Please!" Isobel threw herself on the ground before Andrew. "How can you treat us so?"

Justine felt sickened by her attempt to play on Andrew's sympathies.

"I have been ill-used," she continued to cry. "Darren has—"

"Don't believe her!" Darren stormed. "This was her idea, from the very beginning. I went along with it—"

"I don't care whose idea it was," Andrew said coldly. "How can I do this you ask? You were planning to murder the woman I am to marry. Not to mention my future sister-in-law, brother-in-law, my best friend and a Bow Street runner. You also killed Celia, I've no doubt. I have no pity for you, Isobel."

Isobel's teary eyes flared with venomous anger. "They deserved to die! I should be a marchioness! I—"

Andrew leaned forward. "Prison or exile? I need your final decision, or I shall make the choice myself." His face was rock-hard with disdain.

For a heartbeat, Isobel glared at Andrew. Then she sagged. "I will agree. We'll leave the country."

Andrew nodded. "Fine. We will say nothing—as long as you stay away from all of us, and threaten no one else. You must leave England by this time tomorrow. Remember, for ten years at the very least."

Isobel nodded, stood up, and turned away, her shoulders bent with defeat.

Andrew inclined his head toward Edward, and

Edward and the others released Darren and the two men, their hands still bound.

"What about our hands?" asked Darren, in a subdued voice.

"Ask your sister to untie you at home," Andrew shot back.

"How dare you try to implicate me," Darren muttered as he caught up to Isobel.

"You swore your plan would work!" she retorted as they moved off, their men scurrying after them.

"You said we had nothing to fear—"

Their argumentative voices drifted away as they moved down the path.

"It would be amusing to come upon them and hear Isobel try to explain their bound hands," Edward remarked with a chuckle.

Justine finally felt able to breathe. She took a deep, shuddery breath of the damp, windy evening air. It smelled of flowers and the promise of rain.

"Kevin!" Charlotte stumbled into her fiancé's arms.

"We shall all immediately write down what occurred tonight," Andrew said, "and give the papers to my solicitors."

Justine took a second, deep breath. She turned to face Andrew.

He reached out and took her hand. His was firm and warm against her cold one. "You are unharmed?" he asked quietly.

She nodded. "Yes." It came out a whisper. What was he thinking, she wondered as she looked into his deep blue eyes.

She had begun to tremble as relief engulfed her—

relief, followed by a strange nervousness. What now? She tried to scrutinize and interpret his expression, but it remained unreadable.

His grip tightened. "Come, Justine," he said, his voice rather gruff. "We will return to Rawlings House. We have much to discuss."

Chapter Sixteen

Rawlings House was quiet when they returned.

During the nearly silent walk home, Justine had been rather numb, barely able to concentrate on anything but the overwhelming relief engulfing her. Relief that Isobel was exposed; and that the sudden danger she had faced was finally over. And gladness that her plan had worked—to a certain extent.

It was obvious that Andrew had been alerted to her plan—most likely by Edward—and that was why he had been there. And most fortunate for all of them that he had been alerted.

Edward and the runner had followed Isobel and her party at a discreet distance to make sure they went directly back to Isobel's home. Justine had no doubt that the mortified Isobel and her brother would speedily exit the country.

But as she, Andrew, Kevin and Charlotte neared Rawlings, the reality of her situation began to set in.

During the commotion, she had given away her true feelings. She had said aloud that she loved Andrew. And he could not have missed hearing it by any stretch of the imagination.

The question was, how did he feel?

And what would he do, now that the danger was over? Would they continue their pretend betrothal?

Was there any possibility—dear Heaven—that he would wish to marry her because in his heart lurked an affection?

A fine rain began to fall as they reached her home.

Justine cleared her throat. "Ask our butler to show you to the library," she said. "I will be there in a moment."

Justine and Charlotte slipped inside by the rose gardens, leaving Andrew and Kevin to make their way to the front.

They were able to creep in unobserved. The sisters quickly shed their cloaks, then Charlotte hurried to the front parlor to meet Kevin. Justine walked down the corridor to the library and slipped inside, hoping for a moment to compose herself.

Her heart was still hammering, and her throat was dry.

She tried to breathe deeply, willing her pounding heart to slow its beat.

The clock ticked, once again seeming unusually loud. She was unsuccessful in calming herself. She felt as much on edge now as she had when she went to meet Isobel.

Within two minutes she heard Andrew's firm footsteps along with their butler's.

"Miss Justine?" The butler sounded puzzled. As well

he should be, since she had disappeared upstairs several hours ago saying she wanted to be left undisturbed.

"Yes."

"Lord Andrew Pennington, the Marquis of Whitbury."

"Show him in." Justine inclined her head, and Andrew entered the room.

The butler bowed and exited, leaving the door partly ajar.

Andrew stared at Justine, his expression stern as Danver's footsteps faded away.

She felt her heart plummet to the floor.

"Justine." His voice was crisp. His eyes held hers. "Whatever were you thinking?"

"What—what do you mean?" she asked, trying to hide her nervousness.

"What were you thinking of to concoct such a plan?"

She swallowed. "I wanted to pursue the idea of trapping Isobel. But I didn't want to wait until you returned. How did you get home so fast?"

Andrew walked over to stand close in front of her. She could see the tension in his face. "I had secretly made my way back towards London in order to try to trap Isobel myself," he said, his voice still strained. "Only Edward knew precisely where I was, and he got word to me as soon as you revealed your plan. Thank goodness he did."

"Yes, it was fortunate," Justine said faintly. Why did he keep staring at her so intently? Whatever was he thinking?

She did not have to wait long to find out.

"Don't you know how dangerous your scheme was?" he said, his voice rising. "Did you not realize the peril you were in?"

"I felt I had no choice," Justine said. Her hands clenched. "It was imperative that I trap Isobel. I knew there could be danger, yes; but I was sure that with Edward and the runner and Kevin nearby, no harm would come to me."

"It bloody well came close," Andrew muttered, turning away and staring out the window as rain pinged against the glass. The window was partially open, and a draft whisked through the air, making the candles flicker. Shadows skimmed the wall.

"Why did you not wait 'til I returned?" His voice was curt.

"I—" Justine could not be dishonest. It was time for the truth, she decided. Slowly, she continued. "I wanted—needed—to know how you felt about me. With Isobel incriminated, I thought that . . . you and I . . . must decide whether to continue our arrangement . . . or, perhaps . . ." Her throat seemed to be closing up. She looked away, watching a candle flame bend in the draft, and donned her courage like a cloak. This might be her only chance to make the suggestion. "Perhaps . . . consider turning this into a true betrothal," she finished softly.

Andrew was silent for a moment. And another.

Justine's heart seemed to be wedged high in her throat. She turned her head back to him, and saw Andrew was looking straight at her.

"Did you really mean what you said to Isobel and

Darren?" He asked the question quietly, his eyes holding hers.

There could be no denial.

"Yes," she whispered.

In two strides he had reached her and pulled her into his arms.

"Jus-tine." His voice broke on her name. "Oh, Justine—" And his lips came down on hers.

Justine's head whirled as he kissed her. Her arms went around him as he pulled her even closer. She felt as if lightning bolts raced through her as Andrew kissed her, his kiss growing hard and more demanding.

She clung to him, her heart and soul reeling.

After another minute, he lifted his head, freeing her lips. Hers burned. He continued to hold her tightly.

"Justine," he whispered simply. "Justine . . . I love you too."

"Oh! Oh—Andrew!" Pure happiness shot through her. And she found herself engulfed in his kiss once more.

The chimes on the grandfather clock in the hall finally penetrated the haze surrounding them both. Andrew released her lips and smiled down at Justine, still holding her tightly.

"I will have to keep an eye on you after we are married, my darling," he said, his voice not quite steady. "I do not want to see you get involved in any more schemes. It is my aim to keep you safe—always."

"I do not want to be involved in any other schemes," Justine said, smiling up at her beloved, joy shimmering through her. "I only did it so you would not end our betrothal, as you had suggested. I felt my heart would break if you did. I knew I loved you and wanted to be your wife, and was hoping that perhaps, in time, you would feel the same way."

"I did—but did not realize it until recently." Andrew loosened his grip on her waist so that he could take her hands and kiss them. "And I became determined to truly make you my wife." He pulled her into his arms again.

They kissed for long moments. Every limb of her body sang with happiness.

He pulled away, and suddenly, Andrew dropped to one knee. "I must do this properly!" he declared, his eyes gleaming, his mouth smiling widely. "Justine, will you do me the honor of becoming my wife? In truth?"

"Yes," she whispered breathlessly, smiling down at the man she adored. "Oh, yes!"

He stood and kissed her again. Then he touched her face lightly. "Justine . . . we shall be married soon, my dearest, and then I shall be hard pressed to let you out of my sight."

"That is fine with me." Justine smiled up at him, thrills sweeping through her at his returning grin. "I shall enjoy being your wife."

"A marchioness, no less."

"What Isobel wanted enough to kill for." Justine shivered as she said the words.

Andrew admonished, "Don't think about her. Think about us. You shall be a splendid marchioness."

"I would marry you if you were simply Mr. Pennington," she added, lacing her fingers through his and tightening them. "I love you. And we shall be very happy."

"True." He bent his head again. "And I love you, too, Justine. Now, come give your future husband the marquis, another kiss, right this very minute."

And as the clock ticked quietly, their lips met in a kiss that declared their everlasting love.